"Last night I saved your life."

Her eyes swept over him. "When you were bringing the horse out of the fire, he crunched you by the barn door," she told him tautly. "You fell just inside the door. How do you think you got outside? I want repayment."

Jordan's eyes narrowed, and he pulled her close, as if to get a better look. "What kind of repayment?"

Kara closed her eyes, remembering the way she'd cradled his head in her arms, willing him to live. She forced the soft, breathless note out of her voice. "I want Dad out of jail. And I want you to let us rebuild that barn."

"I'm not sure my life's worth *that* much." He swore under his breath and half turned away from her, then swung back. He swore again....

Peggy Nicholson, daughter of a Texas wildcatter, comes by her risk-taking naturally. Despite a fear of heights, she has dabbled in rock climbing and has been known to climb scaffolding to repaint her Rhode Island home when needed. She's been a teacher, an artist and a restorer of antique yachts. But her two main passions are sailing and writing, which, she insists, are all the better when combined. As Peggy says, ''I can't imagine a nicer way to live.''

Look for Peggy's quick witted charmer of a story 'Hartz and Flowers,' in Harlequin's short-story collection, *Be My Valentine*, in retail stores for February. She delivers a hero who's bound to win your heart!

Books by Peggy Nicholson

HARLEQUIN ROMANCE
3009—TENDER OFFER

HARLEQUIN PRESENTS
732—THE DARLING JADE
741—RUN SO FAR
764—DOLPHINS FOR LUCK

HARLEQUIN SUPERROMANCE
193—SOFT LIES, SUMMER LIGHT
237—CHILD'S PLAY
290—THE LIGHT FANTASTIC

BURNING DREAMS

Peggy Nicholson

Harlequin Books

TORONTO • NEW YORK • LONDON
AMSTERDAM • PARIS • SYDNEY • HAMBURG
STOCKHOLM • ATHENS • TOKYO • MILAN

ISBN 0-373-03100-9

Harlequin Romance first edition January 1991

To Maggie and Erwin Grimes,
who taught me how to dream
and how to make dreams come true.
Who gave me Spice the cow pony,
and when I survived her,
gave me Topper—
now there was a horse!

CHAPTER ONE

"THIS TIME he's gonna do it!" Bill Brody announced the moment Kara opened the door. He swayed, bumped into the doorjamb, then grabbed hold of it to hold himself up. "Hank's really gonna do it, Kara."

Wrinkling her nose at the smell of stale beer, Kara Tate clutched her terry cloth bathrobe together below her throat. "Do what?" she demanded, though somehow she knew already. Attracted to the light inside her motel room, a candlefly swooped out of the soft Texas night. Her stomach swooped and fluttered along with it.

"He's gonna burn Stonehall's barn! Hank got to complaining, like he does when he's down. And that damned Bubba Hendricks told Hank he was sick and tired of hearing about that damned barn and that damned one-eyed horse and those lying, cheating, lousy Stonehalls. He said that if your dad was any kind of man, he'd have done something about the way he was cheated years ago—if he really was cheated."

"That fat little creep!" Kara cried indignantly. "If he wants to go stirring up trouble, I'll give him trouble!" She turned back into the room. "Come on in while I get dressed, Bill."

"Oh, Bubba stirred up trouble all right," Bill drawled behind her. "He brought a bottle of Jack Daniels over to our table."

Kara swung around. "Bill, you let Dad drink *bourbon*?" Bill knew what hard liquor did to her father! That was why Hank stuck to beer on the rare occasions when he went out drinking with the boys. He was still living down that Christmas party at Caswell's Paint and Hardware three years ago. Everybody agreed afterward that the eggnog had been a killer, but it was her father who'd put on the Santa suit and stolen the plastic reindeer and gone out tap dancing. On top of somebody's car.

And there was that time he'd helped console Alf Edwards, when Alf's first child turned out to be triplets. They'd taken a notion for tacos, and next think Kara knew, he'd been calling her from a jail in Piedras Negras, Mexico. Something about mooning the chief of police....

"Yep, Bubba stirred up a potful of trouble," Bill agreed. "He said if Hank really wanted to burn down that barn, he had a full gasoline can out in his pickup Hank could use."

Kara's heartbeat was suddenly loud in her own ears. "Dad's got *gasoline*? Wh-where is he, Bill?"

"I reckon he's halfway to Stonehall's by now." The tall roofer sat down on Kara's bed suddenly and put his head in his hands. "Hooo," he muttered under his breath. "Guess I had one too many, myself."

"I can see that!" After two years of doing remodeling together, she knew Bill like a brother—thought of him as one. But he'd sure botched things tonight. "Where are your truck keys?" Rushing to him, Kara hovered impatiently while he searched his nearest jeans pocket. "You were going to look out for him, Bill, darn you!" He explored his other pocket with maddening slowness. "Why didn't you stop him?"

"Stop him? With Bubba all but callin' him a coward to his face? And Wilson Norman saying fifty'd get you a hundred that Hank would never do it? So Eddy up and says he has a hundred right here that says Hank's no coward. He said he'd bet a hundred any ol' day that Hank'd put his matches where his mouth is, and Hank could even use his blow torch if he wanted."

With friends like that, who needed enemies? She smacked his knee so hard he yelped in protest. "Where are your *keys*, Bill?"

He gave her an injured look. "If they ain't here, reckon they're in the truck. You mean to go out to Stonehall's?"

"What do you think?"

Flogging Bill's ancient pickup up and down the cedar and oak covered hills that gradually rose from the town of Kerrville toward the Stonehall ranch, Kara murmured a chant of pleas and threats to her absent parent. "Dad, you're not going to do it! I won't let you do it. You *can't* do it." For the past ten years, whenever life threatened to topple over on him, Hank Tate would say that he ought to burn the barn down; that the Stonehall's barn had been the start of all his troubles. And maybe it had been, but if he burned it down, Jordan Stonehall would be on him like a hawk on a quail chick.

Jordan Stonehall. She'd only met him that once, ten years ago. At the time she'd only been ten to his twenty, but she still remembered the way he'd looked her up and down, as she stood with her back to the door to Smoky Joe's stall.

"You've got a horse of mine, there," he'd said quietly. His face had been expressionless, but somehow she'd recognized the anger behind those stone-gray eyes. "Mind stepping aside and letting me see him?"

Something about those eyes made her hug herself, as if doing so would protect her from their light touch on her skin. She shook her head stubbornly. "He's not your horse! Your dad gave him to my dad for building him a barn."

"He did, shortstuff, but it was all a mistake. My dad forgot I own a quarter share in Smoky Joe's dam. I planned his breeding myself. I want him back." He took a long step closer.

"Y-y-you can't have him back!" she stuttered, her hand moving to the latch on the stall door one moment before his own hand closed around it. She squeaked with horror at the cool touch of his fingers, and snatched her hand away, but still she wouldn't back down.

He smiled then and really looked at her. If his gaze had been like a brushing of fingertips before, now it was like a piercing. Skewered on the cold, gray point of it, she'd returned his look helplessly. "I'm not going to take him for nothing, sweetheart." For some reason his voice gentled as his eyes grew sharper. "I'll pay you good money for him. But Joe wasn't bred to be a kid's pony. He's going to be a racehorse someday."

"He's going to be *our* racehorse," she insisted. "That's why we want him."

His eyes narrowed and turned stone cold. "*You* all mean to race him? And who the dev—Who's going to train him, then? Your dad?" When she nodded defiantly, he laughed, but it was an angry laugh. He shook his head and slammed an open palm into the door frame above her head, making her jump. "Well, if that doesn't take the cake!" he growled under his breath. "And I suppose you'll be the jockey, shortstuff?"

Stonehall must have read the answer in her eyes. He laughed again, and this time his laugh was genuine. That made it hurt all the more. "You'd better do some fast growing, then, half-pint. Joe wouldn't stop till you two hit Mexico City, if you tried to ride him."

She opened her mouth to deny it, to say that Joe would already let her ride him around his stall, when she saw her father's truck bumping into the yard. Instead she ducked under Stonehall's elbow and ran for it.

When she and Hank returned to the barn, her dad explained, first with the courtesy due his employer's only son, and then with growing indignation, that Smoky Joe was not for sale—not for any price.

The men talked till there was nothing left to say, neither of them ever raising his voice and neither of them giving an inch. Finally Stonehall had said, "All right, then. But I'd like to see him before I go." The words were phrased as a request, but there was no question of denying him. Kara and her father waited outside their shabby little barn as if they were the trespassers while Stonehall went into Joe's stall alone.

When he came out again, he touched the brim of his Stetson to Kara as if she were a grown woman instead of a kid, but the look in his eyes froze her bones. That look said, we're not done yet, girl. Not by a long shot. Then he turned and strode away, long-legged and lithe in the twilight.

And the very next day after Stonehall had been left alone with Joe, Joe had taken to rubbing one side of his face against the water bucket in his stall. The day after that, he'd started crying from that eye. And by the end of the week, Kara had realized Joe no longer walked a straight line. He drifted always to the right, as if this were the one safe path in a world gone strange and fearsome. Smoky Joe had gone blind in one eye.

As her pickup topped a hill with an almost human wheeze, Kara spotted a pair of taillights ahead. "Dad!" But when she neared the lights, she saw this was a car, not the five-year-old Chevy truck her father had bought last week. That Chevy had taken every last cent they'd just finished earning on the motel remodeling job. But they'd had no

choice but to buy it—their faithful old van had quietly hic-
cuped and died on its way to the grocery store.

"Was that what did it, Dad?" Was that what made him
snap, at last? Because Hank had had all kinds of plans and
dreams for that motel money. Kara gritted her teeth,
stamped down on the gas and overtook the car ahead, not
with a rush, but with a creeping, rattling determination that
caused the other car to give way grudgingly and let her
rumble to the lead.

Or maybe he'd snapped because Bill and Eddy were leaving the team after two years of practically being family. Tonight's jaunt to the bar had been something between a
farewell celebration and a wake to mark the end of the
partnership. Bill and Eddy were moving on to Dallas, taking their roofing and plumbing skills with them. Without the
guys, Tate Remodeling would be nothing but a small-time,
small-town, father and daughter handyman operation. "But
still, Dad, ending up in jail isn't going to make things any
better!"

Of course, he'd been saying he ought to burn the barn
down for years. But that didn't mean he'd really go through
with it. Hank Tate was probably back in Kerrville, telling
any fool who'd listen how the Stonehalls had cheated him
out of the greatest racing stud Texas had ever bred.

"Ten thousand dollars," Kara murmured bitterly, as she
roared past the stone pillar that marked the start of Stonehall land. That was what Jordan Stonehall had given her
father to buy back Smoky Joe. And at the time, that had
seemed like the best of a bad bargain to her father, for what
use was a half-blind Thoroughbred?

Well, Jordan Stonehall had shown him what use! Smoky
Joe didn't race till he was four—it took that long to train
him to run on faith alone. But by the time he retired to a life

of bawdy ease as top stud of the Stonehall's breeding program, he'd become a living legend.

And her father was pointed out around town as another kind of local landmark. He was the poor, crazy fool who'd traded a gold mine like Smoky Joe for ten thousand measly dollars.

The truck swung around the final bend, and up ahead Kara could see the stone arch that marked the drive to Stonehall's ranch. She'd never seen it, but Dad had described it to her many times. "You and me should be living in a place like that, Kara! If we hadn't been robbed..." She turned the truck under the arch in a cloud of dust, rocks rattling under the tires, and stormed up the long hill.

"Oh, don't be here, Dad. Please don't be here!" The road was surprisingly narrow, fenced to right and left with walls of Texas field stone. Ancient liveoaks overhung it, their dark, glossy leaves shutting out the stars. As she neared the top of the hill, headlights lit the ridge and the leaves overhead, then raked down to shine in her eyes. Kara stomped on the brakes, and the pickup died. A truck slid to a halt in a cloud of dust, its headlights eyeball to eyeball with those of her pickup. "Dad?" She squinted against the light.

"Get out of the way!" a man yelled. His voice was hoarse, slurred with panic or booze, and very familiar.

"Eddy?" Kara slid out of the truck. "Eddy, where's Dad?"

The driver leaned over Eddy and the man between them to yell at her. "Get outa the way, damn it! We gotta get out of here!"

She glared at him. "Bubba Hendricks, you tell me where my dad is!"

The small, chubby man jerked back from the window as he recognized her. "Why, Kara!" He gave her a shaky smile.

"What are you doin' out here? And in your bathrobe? That ain't to say you don't look great in a bath—"

"Bubba Hendricks!" On tiptoe, Kara leaned through the truck window. "I don't need any of your soft soaping tonight!" she cried passionately. "I know what you started, and now I'm going to finish it! Where's Dad?"

"Uh, he's back there." Bubba jerked his chin at the road behind.

"We got to get out of here!" the man between Bubba and Eddy proclaimed. "Forget the bet, I don't want no part of this! Tell that turkey to get out of the road!" Apparently thinking there was a driver in Kara's pickup, he jammed his hand down on the truck horn, and held it down.

"Enough of this!" Kara announced, though none of the men could hear her. She ran around to Bubba's side of the truck and hammered on his arm that rested on the window frame. "Back up, Bubba! I've got to get by you!"

"We're gonna get in trouble, Kara," he warned her. "If Stonehall catches us—"

"You haven't even *begun* to see trouble, if you don't get out of my way!" She hammered his arm again till he winced. "Now move!"

Teeth clamped together, pounding on her pickup's steering wheel with frustration, she followed them as they retreated at the pace of a dying turtle up the long hill. Twice Bubba crunched into the stone walls to either side, then had to pull forward, straighten out and continue backing.

As she waited on the crest for Bubba's pickup to back into the narrow pull-off just below, she glanced in her rearview mirror. At the foot of the hill, headlights gleamed and danced through the oak leaves as another vehicle swung through the archway. But she had no time to wonder who that could be. Stomping on the gas, she passed Bubba's truck with a clattering roar. In her rearview mirror, she saw him pull out and disappear over the hilltop. In a minute or two, he'd be headlight to headlight with whoever was coming. Maybe with practice, his backing up would improve.

The road led downhill, along a valley thick with gigantic oaks, over a hump-backed stone bridge that spanned a creek, then up a higher hill. Just below its crest, at the top of a long meadow, stood the stone house, sheltered from the north wind, master of all it surveyed. It was not the castle she'd always imagined when her father rambled on about the Stonehall's riches. It was one of the lovely old German ranchhouses from the 1800s, built like a little fort, its only exterior gracenote the second-floor balcony that extended across its width. Its stones would be golden by daylight.

The barn her father built rose out of a cup-shaped hollow a quarter mile beyond the house. It wasn't as big as Kara had always pictured it, though it was big enough. It had reared over her whole life like an evil, unseen monster. If her father had never built this barn... With a shudder, she stopped the pickup by Hank's Chevy truck. The wide barn doors stood open, and yellow light cast a long rectangle out into the dark stable yard. A horse whickered somewhere nearby. "Joe," she whispered, though that was ridiculous. Stonehall must own half a hundred horses besides Joe.

Only one light near the entrance had been switched on, but as she stepped into the barn, it showed her the dim outlines of the center aisle. An open door on her right led to an office. She saw books, file cabinets, a battered desk, shelves of trophies. A horseshoe-shaped wreath of dried roses, big enough for a racehorse to wear around its neck, arched across one wall.

The door opposite the office led to a tack room. She breathed in the clean, rich smell of saddle soap. "Dad?"

Deeper within the building, tall double doors stood open. Kara looked into a single large room, which took up the rest of the space on this side of the barn. A breeding arena, she guessed and turned away.

Across the center aisle of the barn, the top half of a wide stall door stood open. Her nostrils flared with the warm, earthy scent of manure, then a horse nickered again. Suddenly she was sure. "Joe?" She caught the bars with both hands and pressed her face between them.

A soft *"Hah!"*, a comment and a snort all at once, greeted her, then something large and pale moved restlessly on the far side of the roomy box stall.

"Joe, where's Dad?"

The stud snorted again, and even in the darkness, she could see the whites of his eyes roll. Something had spooked him—Hank? Kara turned, and froze as she saw the gas can.

It sat on the floor in front of the next stall. Quickly she went to it, caught its handle and tried to shake it. It was too heavy to lift one-handed. She breathed a heartfelt sigh of relief. Thank God, it was still full. But why had he left it here? And where was he?

There were only two more stalls in the barn, and both were empty. Which made sense, a breeding stallion was often stabled separately. But if there were no other horses here but Joe, where was her father?

Somewhere a cat mewed, then a familiar voice mumbled.

"Dad!" she called, this time not caring who heard her.

She was rewarded by a distant gasp. *"Kara?"* His voice came from somewhere above. "What are you doing here, girl?"

Peering up into the loft, she could make out a flickering reflection of light. It shimmered over bales of hay stacked to the rafters and bounced off the roof beams. Oh, God, was that fire? "Dad!"

But he didn't answer this time. Across the aisle, a stairway climbed into the shadows. It resounded hollowly as she bounded up it. "Dad!"

Up in the loft, hay was stacked higher than her head, and the heat settled over her like a prickly wool blanket. She ducked around a wall of hay and there he was at last, sitting on a bale, Eddy's portable blow torch burning merrily in one hand. A very large tiger cat wove back and forth before him, rubbing its back against his shins. "Dad," she said soothingly as she glided closer, "what do you think you're doing?"

His eyes were too bright even for firelight. They smiled at her then drifted on by, taking in the walls, then the rafters above. "I built this," he told her, waving the torch to encompass it all, while he wiped the tears off his cheeks with his free hand.

"I know." He looked like an awed cherub, come to the cathedral for the first time, rather than an avenging angel. The torch's flame reflected off his bald head, and sitting, he looked even smaller than he was.

"Just me and a team of six men, I built this. I bet it's the only post and beam barn in all of Texas." He shook his head, smiled, and more tears dripped down his face. "I told Ol' Man Stonehall he was crazy, wanting post and beam. I'd never even built one, though my daddy had, back in Massachusetts. But once that ol' cuss got a notion in his head..." He shook his head, in admiration or sorrow, it was impossible to say which. "We had to go all the way to East Texas to get the wood. She's oak and long-leaf yellow pine, and cedar for the skin."

"I know, Daddy." He'd told her a thousand times before. Eyeing the propane torch, Kara edged closer, and the cat flowed to meet her.

Hank Tate leaned forward, idly aiming the torch at the loft floor. The blue jet of deadly flame danced only inches above a wisp of straw. "And we used some cypress for the floor planks," he said matter-of-factly. "I'd forgotten that."

Should she simply dive for the torch? But with the cat underfoot, she'd be tripped for sure. "Careful with that flame," she murmured instead. "You don't want to burn her."

He nodded, stood and moved away from her, his steps unsteady in the flickering light. "I thought I did, Kara, but I can't. This is the best thing—this is the *only* worthwhile thing—I ever built in my whole life."

Tears stung at the back of her own eyes, and she shook her head till her ash-blond hair fanned out in the torch-light. "That's not true, Dad! What about those houses over on Amarillo Street?" She could have bitten her tongue as soon as she said it.

He swung around wildly, the torch flaring as he turned, his black, grizzly eyebrows pulled up into anguished peaks. "Don't remind me!"

He'd taken the ten thousand given him for Smoky Joe and invested it in a little subdivision of houses, built on speculation. About the time he and his partner had completed the houses, interest rates had shot through the roof. When the rates rose, they couldn't sell, and they couldn't keep up with the construction loan. The bank foreclosed. And the biggest stockholder in the Kerrville bank had been Jordan Stonehall's father.

And then, to complete the chain of awful luck, Kara's mother had died soon after that.

Her father's thoughts must have been paralleling her own. He jabbed the torch toward the ceiling, Job cursing the sky. "It's a bad-luck barn, that's what it is! *Somebody* ought to burn it, if I can't!"

"No." She caught his wiry forearm. "No, Dad, it doesn't need burning. It's too beautiful." She'd spoken the words to pacify him, but even as she said them, they echoed in her mind with the clear, pure ring of truth. No matter what trouble it had caused, this barn wasn't evil. Beyond the circle of the torchlight, she could feel the structure rising around her into the darkness, a shape of symmetry and rugged grace. A link with a carpenter grandfather she'd never known.

Tears streaming down his cheeks, Hank turned a slow circle and stared upward in childlike wonder. "She is beautiful, isn't she?"

"I've never seen anything like her!"

He nodded dreamily. "You're right. I'll never build anything like her again. All these years of laying linoleum and stripping wallpaper and putting in toilets... Building a godforsaken doghouse, for Pete's sake... All the time, at the back of my head, I'm saying, but I built *this*! Once upon a time, I built *one* thing that'll last. This baby'll still be standing when you're a grandma, Kara."

Kara reached across him and gently took the torch from his hand. "You'll build other things as beautiful, Dad."

He shook his head, then ducked it suddenly to swipe his sleeve across his eyes. "Me and who else, Kara? You, baby?" He laughed shakily. "I don't even have a crew anymore! I've run out of time. I'll be sixty next week—it just hit me tonight. Sixty and what have I got to show for it?"

So that was what had set him off. Tucking her arm through his, she tugged him toward the stairs. "You've got me," she reminded him.

"I don't deserve you," he mumbled, bumping into her as they walked. "And I shouldn't have you. You ought to be off in college, dating boys and having a good time. Not helping me paint houses. That's no life."

Kara sighed and didn't try to answer that. She'd tried going off to the state university once—she'd won almost a full scholarship—but it hadn't worked out. Without her for company, her dad had gotten so blue that she'd refused to go back the next year. They rounded a stack of bales, the barn cat tagging at their heels. "Did you see Joe downstairs?" she asked, to distract him.

"Yeah, him and me had a long talk. I've been meaning to tell that ol' devil for years what I think of him. If he'd had any decency, he'd have sat down in the middle of the racetrack, 'stead of running like a damned house on fire for the Stonehalls."

Kara laughed softly. They reached the top of the stairs, and Hank stopped. "Look at this, Kara." He pointed overhead, to where a cross beam joined a vertical post. "Want to show you how we fastened her together. See that wooden peg?" He took the torch from her hand and held it overhead. "That's a treenail—trunnel they call 'em. That's what they used before they had nails and bolts. Ol' man Stonehall was a stickler for details like that." His head swung as he followed the big side beam to where it disappeared behind the stacked hay. "And—oh! You've got to see this!" He caught her hand and dragged her after him.

Kara hung back. "Don't you think we should go, Dad? What if Stonehall catches us here?"

"Huh!" Hank said rudely, and stopped as a wall of hay blocked the way. "I'm not afraid of Jordan Stonehall, any more than I was of his ol' man. And his daddy was so ornery, I can't figure what killed him." Ducking down, he set the torch on the beam that ran at knee height the length of the barn and started shifting bales of hay. The cat ducked between his legs and disappeared between two bales.

"I know it's here someplace." Hank moved another bale of hay to the side, stacked a third on top of it. The stack teetered and Kara put a hand up to steady it. Moving into the gap he'd created, Hank ran his hand along the beam. "A little further along," he mumbled, and moved the torch along the top of the beam to give himself more light. He shifted another bale.

Somewhere ahead, a high-pitched, demanding *mew!* sounded, then another. "She's got kittens in there!" Kara laughed and crowded closer.

"Yeah," Hank agreed absently and lifted yet another bale. Three more feet of beam were now exposed.

"There they are!" Hank's efforts had also revealed a cozy nest, hollowed out of a bale that had burst its binding wire. The tiger cat lay regally outstretched, two tiny kittens kneading her creamy belly fur. The cat's eyes narrowed as Hank picked up the torch.

"Here it is! Just look at this, Kara." He brought the torch flame near the beam.

In the stark light, the numbers stood out black and bold. The date 1980 had been routed into the wood. Beside that in smaller letters was carved a list of seven men, her father's name at the top.

Hank chuckled to himself. "Jake Harris— I haven't thought of him in years! That man could cut the prettiest mortises you ever saw." His fingertip stroked another name. "And big Ike. He could just about raise a bent single-handed. He went to California, I believe."

Kara waited while he savored the memories, his finger brushing back and forth across the letters. Finally he sighed and traced the date again. "Nineteen eighty! Somebody'll come along a hundred years from now and see that, they'll hardly believe it. But here we are, forever and ever. Yes sir, we built this. We built this mighty fine." He set the torch on the beam, patted the wood farewell, then turned to the cat.

"Well, mama, you got a nice family there," he crooned. The cat had left her kittens. She sat licking herself nervously, while the kittens nuzzled the straw and called for her. Bending down, Hank scooped up the kittens and turned. "Look at these critters. They haven't even opened their eyes yet." He held the squirming pair out to Kara.

Kara laughed as she reached for them. "I don't know if you should—"

He shouldn't have. The mama cat sprang at his leg, dug in her claws and started climbing Hank like a tree. Stomping like a flamenco dancer, Hank whirled around, the climbing cat adding its moaning snarl to his yelps of pain and the kittens' terrified squeals. His elbow hit the torch.

"Dad!" Kara lunged for it as it went flying into the cat nest. But Hank spun after it too, and they collided. Knocked backward, Kara thumped into the tower of bales beside her. They toppled onto Hank and the torch.

"No!" she screamed. An ominous crackling sounded from under the heap, and a wisp of smoke twisted toward the rafters.

Pinned from his waist down Hank held the squeaking kittens aloft. With a strength she'd never known she had, Kara tossed a bale aside. *"Where's the torch?"* The wisp of smoke was thickening to a torrent.

"C-can't see it," Hank coughed. "Where's the damn cat?"

But that was the least of their worries. Kara lifted a final bale, and saw the torch. In the midst of a spreading pool of flame, one side of it glowed cherry red. On its fuel canister, the word *propane* blackened and burned as she stared at it, then the meaning of that word registered. She slammed the bale back in place, a split second before the explosion.

Sheets of flame whooshed sideways between the bales. A wall of fire reared toward the rafters. With a shriek Kara grabbed her father and ran.

Heat, smoke, terror, Hank's stumblebum feet—she had no conscious thoughts, only fleeting images of flames rippling along the bales overhead, blinding smoke, the blessed stairs underfoot, then the coolness of concrete beneath her bare soles. Hank tripped, fell, and she pulled him up as if he were no weight at all. Then they were staggering out the barn door. Coughing, rubbing at her eyes, Kara could hear crickets singing out in the darkness, and the crackle of flames behind. And a horse screaming.

"Joe!" Whirling around, she clamped her hands to her ears and backed slowly away from the horror. "Oh, *no*, Daddy, not Joe!"

"I'll get him!" Hank turned to the doors, took a step forward, then stopped. The interior of the barn was already bright with dancing flames.

"No!" Kara caught his arm with both hands. "No, you can't do that, Dad!"

The stallion screamed again, and her father shook her off, then turned to thrust the kittens into her hands. "Yes, I can, baby," he told her hoarsely. He jerked his chin toward the burning barn. "If I can do this, then at least I can do that." He pushed her back a step. "I have to," he said pleadingly.

"No!"

"Yes." He swung her around and planted a hand between her shoulderblades, shoving her so hard she almost fell. "Now go get help!" he yelled after her.

"No!" she sobbed as she staggered to a halt. She spun back, her hair and her robe flaring around her. "No!" she begged, but he was gone into that billowing smoke as if he'd never been.

CHAPTER TWO

GET HELP. But they were twenty miles from Kerrville's fire trucks. A ranch this big must have its own fire-fighting equipment, but where it was or how to use it, she didn't know. "Oh, God, oh Daddy, oh, God!" She backed away another step, staring into the smoke. She would have to go in there. He wasn't any good with horses. Never had been.

No, it was up to her. Running to the nearest truck, she tucked the squalling kittens in the back. They'd be safe there. *Safe—oh, Daddy!* She spun around, then the growl of a motor coming fast spun her back again.

A car was bucketing down the hillside. With one headlight smashed in, it looked like a shiny, winking monster. Sobbing with relief, Kara ran to meet it. Brakes screeched and it slid to a dust-raising halt, its hood nudging her with its final momentum so that she fell forward, her hands braced on its hot smoothness. "Help," she murmured, staring through the windshield into the dark interior.

"Help," she gasped again, as the door whipped open, and the driver swung out of the Jaguar.

"Sweet, *jumping*—" He slammed the car's door with a viciousness that cut through her hysteria. Kara straightened and backed away from him, then squeaked as he followed in one giant's step. He caught the lapels of her robe and yanked her back on tiptoe. "Is anybody in there?" he snarled. His deep-set eyes were incredulous, blazing with sparks reflected from the roof of the burning barn. They skimmed over her firelit body and came back to her face. She nodded and he shook her. "Who? Where?"

"M-m-my dad," she told him, teeth chattering. "He went after Joe. We have to go help—"

"Not we, shortstuff." He dragged her toward the door of his car. "Get in and stay there."

"No, I have to—"

"You have to do what I say."

She shook her head wildly. Somehow Stonehall's arrival had restored her courage. It was her fault this had happened. She had to—

He caught the ends of the sash that hung from her robe and yanked her closer to the car. "What?" she yelped, but he simply shook his head in disgust, his hands looping something through the open window and around the door frame. He gave a final yank, and she bumped up against the door.

"Now stay there," he growled and charged away.

Automatically, she tried to follow and came up short against her tether. He'd tied her sash to the door. "Damn you!" she cried as she tugged at it. His long, lean shape ducked low and vanished into the barn. "Damn you, Jordan Stonehall!" Her fingers tore at the knot, but she couldn't keep her eyes on the problem. She kept swinging around to stare at the blazing barn. "Oh, damn you!" she sobbed. If it hadn't been for Stonehall in the first place... If it hadn't been for stupid, macho pride... She shook her head in bewilderment. No horse was worth this, not even Joe....

Black and misshapen against the flickering red, a hunched shape staggered out of the doorway. Coughing, swearing, carrying her father draped across his back, Stonehall wobbled away from the barn. He dumped Hank's body near the car and straightened, panting.

"Is he all right?" she cried.

"Fire hasn't reached him yet," he growled and whipped off his shirt.

She stared at his flame-gilded body. Then the meaning of his words hit home as he started back, his shirt clenched in one hand. "Oh, no, Jordan, don't!" But he was gone, striding off into the fire without a backward glance. *"No!"* She lunged against the knotted sash, tightening it more, then beat on the top of his car with frustration. Men! If she lived to be a *thousand*, she'd never— She gave up and turned all her rage on the knot. Anything that man could tie, she could untie.

She tore at the sash. She couldn't have said if it was hours or only seconds later that the last loop pulled free. She retied the sash around her waist with a vicious yank and hurried to her father. "Dad?" She shook him until he groaned. He rolled over on his side, curled himself into a ball and smiled without opening his eyes. Kara straightened with a gasp of relief. Apart from the soot smudges, he looked all right.

She turned toward the fire. How long had Stonehall been in there? Could she go in after him? Moving as if in a dream, she drifted close enough to feel the heat on her cheeks.

But she was saved the terrible choice. "Stand clear!" his voice yelled from out of the murk. The stallion screamed. A few feet inside the door, a shape as pale as smoke writhed into the air, swinging Stonehall's body off the ground as he reared. Kara cried out, but Stonehall came back to earth with a cat's saving grace, his boots lighting inches from the stallion's plunging hooves. He held the stud two-handed, one hand clutching the shirt he'd wrapped around Joe's eyes and one hand gripping the halter. "C'mon, fella."

The stud shook his head savagely and plunged sideways, dragging Stonehall with him. "Easy, big guy, we've made it," Stonehall crooned. But the stud had the cool air of freedom in his flaring nostrils. He didn't rear this time, he simply gathered his hindquarters beneath him and soared forward, carrying his handler with him like a ragdoll dangling out the window of a freight train. The shirt slipped from his face.

"Look out!" Kara cried as Joe swerved away from his blind side. But a sickening crash drowned out her words. Brushing Stonehall off against the doorjamb, the stallion lunged out into the night. He reared again as Kara ran forward, but she didn't look up at the hooves waving over her head.

"Jordan!"

The stallion shot off into the darkness. Kneeling in the blast of heat by the door, Kara ran her fingers helplessly over Stonehall's sweat-drenched chest, slapping his cheek, shaking his shoulders. Her fingers came away smeared with blood. "Oh, Jordan, wake up!"

But she didn't even know if he was alive. He wouldn't be for long, if she left him here. Something heavy fell within the barn, and a blast furnace breath of sparks and smoke rolled over them in a stinging cloud.

She caught at his shoulders, and her fingers slipped over him. He was too wet to get a hold on, and far too heavy. Crying, choking, she whipped her sash off, looping it around his back and under his arms. Taking a grip on the ends, she heaved. He moved an inch, then she tripped and sat down.

But if she could move him once, she could move him again. Inch by inch she fought his solid weight across the stable yard. "One more," she panted. The heat was bearable from here. Lifting his heavy head and shoulders by the sash one last time, she staggered backward, bent double under his weight. She stepped on her robe hem, and collapsed with a yelp, managing to cradle Stonehall's head with her hands as she fell. "Oooff!"

End of the line. Kara simply lay there gasping, staring up at the sky. A thick banner of smoke braided overhead, then billowed up to the brilliant stars. Stonehall's head rested on top of her bare stomach, his soft hair tickling her skin. Was he even alive? *Oh, please.*

Overhead, a meteor blazed across the velvet night. Face upturned to watch its fiery arc, she laughed shakily. Someone was granting her a wish. "Let him live," she murmured, to be formal about it. But she knew already. Her hand crept up his cheek, its roughness scratching strange sensations across her palm. "Live," she commanded him tenderly and brought her fingers to his lips. His breath brushed like damp silk against her skin. She laughed to herself again, but this time it was almost a sob.

She ought to check on Hank, but she couldn't make herself move. And if she stayed there, she might see another shooting star. So she lay back for a while, eyes on the sky, her fingers stroking the soft hair above his brow, but she didn't see any more meteors. She could have used another wish or two, come to think of it.

With that thought, Kara sat up. She managed to pull her robe together beneath Stonehall's heavy head, but otherwise, she didn't stir. She sat there, eyes reflecting the blaze, and watched the roof fall in. She watched the mama cat jump from the truck and move purposefully across the barnyard, head held high, a kitten bumping her chest as she stalked off into the darkness. Kara was still sitting there, one hand resting on his forehead, the other on his bare chest, watching the last of the barn burn itself down to glowing charcoal, when Stonehall's ranch hands came back from town.

BATHED IN THE RUDDY RAYS of the setting sun, the stone house floated on its hill like the golden castle she had imagined as a child. Kara stared up at it in fascination and loathing as she drove up the hill. Would he even be home?

When Stonehall's hands had returned from the wedding of one of their own in town, sometime before dawn this morning, they had bundled Hank, their boss and herself off to the hospital in Kerrville. The last she had seen of Jordan Stonehall, he was groggily refusing a stretcher, then limping away down a corridor, a doctor hovering at one shoulder, a nurse at the other. Not for a Stonehall, the long wait in an emergency room that folks like her father had to endure.

After Hank had at last been admitted for observation, and the burns on her hand had been dressed, Kara had tried to find out how Stonehall was faring. She'd even, she recalled now with an angry laugh, entertained some ridiculous notion of bringing him flowers, once she'd found out where the hospital had lodged him. But Stonehall was gone, a nurse told her when she asked. He'd had X-rays, but if the nurse knew their results, she was not about to discuss them with Kara. All she would say was that Mr. Stonehall had left the hospital before the breakfast trays went around.

Perhaps they'd sent him on to one of the big hospitals in San Antonio. Though she'd noticed a plaque in the lobby that stated a wing of the Kerrville hospital had been donated by his father, Kara doubted that Jordan Stonehall considered the small-town hospital to be quite a five-star establishment. Her mouth twisted bitterly as she chose the fork of the drive that swept in front of his ranch house. But five-star or only three, the hospital had been snooty enough about admitting Hank, since the Tates didn't have health insurance. And she still wasn't sure how they would pay. But now that was the least of her worries.

The hospital had kept Hank until late afternoon, when the doctor had decided he was suffering more from a hangover than smoke inhalation. But while they'd been completing checkout, a county deputy sheriff had arrived. He'd been politely apologetic, but he'd been firm. Hank was wanted for arson, and he was there to arrest him. Kara's pleading hadn't made the least bit of difference.

There was only one man who could stop the proceedings. "Be here, Jordan Stonehall," she muttered through her teeth as she parked her truck before the house. "Just you be here."

The woman who answered Kara's knock on the heavy oak door was Chicana, no taller than Kara, but years older. She looked Kara up and down, and her eyebrows rose.

Kara squared her shoulders. No doubt Jordan Stonehall didn't receive many women dressed in jeans and plain white shirt. But she hadn't realized she'd be calling on Stonehall so soon. She had thought to wait till tomorrow before she approached him. She'd hoped she'd have that much time to figure out how she and Hank were going to make restitution and apology. But apparently the rancher believed in exacting swift and deadly retribution.

"Mr. Stonehall, please?" Her hand climbed to the simple squash blossom necklace she wore, an ornament she'd owned since she was twelve. Its turquoise matched her eyes, and she'd always thought it lucky.

"You wait," the woman told her curtly. She repeated the command with a gesture, as if Kara might not understand English, then turned on her heel and marched away.

Kara waited, tiny shudders of rage and apprehension shivering down her spine. Dad in jail. He should still be in a hospital bed, not bumping shoulders with barroom brawlers or worse, in a crowded cell.

"Come," the woman called from the end of the hall. *And is that how she speaks to Stonehall's guests?* Kara wondered resentfully as she obeyed. She couldn't imagine the woman barking at the kind of elegant female visitor Stonehall must usually entertain.

The woman swung open a heavy door and nodded for her to enter.

The room was a library, lit only by the setting sun shining through French doors that stood open to a verandah. Kara paused, taking in books shelved to the ceiling, framed photos of horses racing neck and neck, the ruby tones of an Oriental rug underfoot. The room was rich but not lavish, utterly comfortable, utterly masculine in its choice of colors and textures. She started at the sound of ice in a glass and swung around.

At the end of the room, Jordan Stonehall sat in a big leather chair next to a cold fireplace. His feet were propped up on a hassock, his tawny head tipped back against the red hide. He set the glass he'd been holding on the table beside his chair. "You'll pardon me if I don't stand."

"Yes," she said, though it hadn't been a question. She found her hand creeping to her necklace again as she came forward across the deep rug. Her indignation was slipping away at the sight of him, and she had nothing else with which to replace it. "You're hurt."

He was dressed in a pair of loose white trousers tied with a drawstring, something a man might wear while he practiced karate. His chest was bare, except for the bandage that encircled it. Against the dusky gold of his skin, the tape looked very white.

He shrugged, or started to, then stopped abruptly. "A bit." He had a soft, heavy shirt slung over his shoulders. As he moved, it slipped off his left shoulder, and she saw the thundercloud bruises and the cast that enclosed his forearm.

She winced. More than a bit. Ribs, arm, anything else? Her eyes moved over him with an almost hungry intentness, but that was the worst of the damage, as far as she could see. There was a raw patch, a burn or a scrape, on his high cheekbone. And just above it, his gray eyes awaited hers. She couldn't tell if the gleam in those eyes was of anger or amusement. All Kara knew as she met them, was that their gazes connected with a tiny jolt that almost made her jump—as if an electric circuit had been completed somewhere, or the jaws of a trap had snapped shut. She needed air, she realized suddenly, as if breathing were no longer an act of unconscious certainty.

"How much do you weigh?" he asked. He had a deep voice, its drawl whiskey smooth, too smooth for this part of the state.

College voice, she thought, with an unexpected twinge of despair. "A hundred and five," she said automatically, then frowned. "Why?"

He smiled, and it was the same smile she'd remembered all these years. His eyes flicked over her. "Maybe you were right. Maybe you would have made a jockey."

So he remembered their confrontation, too. It ought to have embarrassed her, but it didn't somehow. She felt a sudden rush of warmth, as if she'd found a friend lost for ten years. "You've got to let him out," she blurted impulsively. "You can't put him in jail for this!"

His smile faded. "Oh, but I can, shortstuff."

Her chin came up sharply. He had called her that last night, hadn't he? "The name is Kara." So she had been wrong—totally—fooled by something about those eyes, or some sense of possession after holding him last night. There was no kinship here. This was the enemy.

"Kara," he said, rolling the sound of it on his tongue the way he'd test an expensive wine. "Funny to know you so long, and to never know."

She couldn't let him distract her. "You can't put him in jail! This was an accident!"

His eyebrows were darker than his straight, tawny hair, and very level, giving him an almost frowning look even in repose. Now they drew together dangerously. "Accident? He's wanted to do this for years, Kara."

"You knew that?" she gasped, then winced inwardly. She should never have admitted it.

"Oh, I knew, all right."

She had the sudden wild sensation that he could look right through walls if he wanted to. She shook her head, shaking off the notion. If he knew, it was only because everybody talked in a small town, Hank most of all, when his worries got too big for him.

"And there was a bet, wasn't there, last night? That he'd finally do it?" He shook his head in disgust, reached for his glass and drained it, then smacked it down again.

Kara swallowed around the lump rising in her throat. "H-h-how did you—" Her knees were shaking. She needed to sit down suddenly, and did so, in the big chair facing his across the hearth.

"Did you happen to notice my car?" he drawled. "I met your buddies last night—head on." There was no question as to what emotion glittered in his eyes now. "We had a little—umm—discussion, once I'd picked them out of my front grill. Looks like your dad's buddy won his hundred dollars, doesn't it? You need bail money, I'd go to him."

The thought of bail money, of not being able to raise it, set a dust devil to spinning in her stomach. He couldn't do this. "All right, Mr. Stonehall, it was stupid, it was child-ish, it was crazy, it was all of those things, but it wasn't on purpose! Not once he'd thought about it. I was there, and I saw what happened. He was using the plumber's torch to see. And there was this cat—And the gasoline—he never even—"

"He had *gasoline* out there? And a blowtorch?" Stone-hall swore one soft, savage word. "I figured we were talk-ing matches." He shook his head. "He can rot in jail for all I care, Kara. You don't go playing with gas—ever. If he hasn't learned that by now, let him learn it the hard way."

"Please..." She had only made things worse, hadn't she? "Please," she said, hating the word, hating him for the power he had to make her say it. But she had to make him see. "He was drunk. He didn't mean it."

His gray eyes were merciless. "Sober or falling-down drunk, a man's responsible for his actions, Kara. If you dance, you pay the piper."

"Easy for you to talk about paying!" she exploded, bouncing to her feet to stand over him. "Born with a silver spoon in your mouth. And then you got richer with an-other man's racehorse!"

She started to whirl away, to leave him there before she said anything worse, but his hand shot out to grip her wrist, and he spun her back around. "Wait one damned minute! Another man's—" He laughed incredulously. "I gave your father ten thousand for that stud!"

"Ten thousand for the best stud in the country! That was *sooo* generous of you, Mr. Stonehall!"

In spite of her resistance he yanked her closer. "Ten thousand for an unproven, half-blind colt, Kara, that looked like a cross between a mule and an antelope—that was plenty generous! Joe was no best anything when I bought him back. I took the gamble, and your dad took the ten thousand. I can't help it if he didn't have the nerve to hang on to him. And I'm damned if I'll feel sorry for a man who can't make the best of a bad poker hand. You make a mistake, you don't let it ruin your life, Kara. You don't spend the rest of your life whining about what rotten luck you had.''

"But he did have rotten luck!" Her eyes filled as she remembered all the years of her father's struggle—the houses he'd lost when the interest rates rose. How could anyone blame him for that? Then her mother's lapse into illness and death the year after that. How could anyone, even this stone-hearted man before her, have stood up to all that? And then to be the butt of all the jokes about losing Smoky Joe! The wonder was that Hank had stayed smiling and working as long as he had, not that he'd finally snapped!

"He made his luck," Stonehall said flatly. "We all do. If you can't see that, then you're truly your father's daughter."

It was an insult, the way he said it. Teeth clenched, she wrenched her arm backward, determined to break free.

As her struggles jerked him sideways in the chair, he let out a startled grunt, and his grip tightened in bruising reflex. She froze—whatever she'd wanted she hadn't meant to hurt him. Stricken, Kara met his eyes. With a rueful grimace he let his breath out between clenched teeth. Then he jerked downward on her wrist and nodded at the hassock before him. "Sit. I don't like you towering over me, short-stuff."

She forgot her concern for him. "You call me that once more, and I'll—"

He laughed, a low, husky growling laugh that seemed to ripple across her skin. "And you'll what? You're going to beat up on an injured man, sweetheart?"

Unwillingly, her eyes flicked over the bare expanse of his chest and shoulders, then down to the brown fingers curled around her wrist. She'd have about as much chance of beating up on an injured grizzly, and he knew it, darn him. Her eyes came up to find his waiting for her, and again there was that odd little *snap!*—a spark jumping some kind of gap.

He swung his feet off the hassock. "Sit." He pulled her down onto it.

This put them knee to knee. It was too close, and again it affected her breathing. His fingers gentled on her wrist, and their movement along that sensitive spot set all kinds of odd tremors shuddering up the length of her arm. She had to stop thinking about this. Had to think how she was going to rescue Hank. She'd had a scrap of a plan before his arrest drove it out of her mind, and she grasped at it now. "You spoke about paying. That's what we want to do, of course..."

"I'm sure my insurance company will be happy to hear that," he drawled lazily. "I had that barn insured for fifty thousand."

Her heart sank. There was no question of raising that kind of money—or even a tenth of it! And if Stonehall was to be reimbursed for it already, then there was no incentive for him to want what she was offering. But it was all she had. "Of course we can't raise that kind of money. But we could rebuild it for you. We could make you a barn just as good as that one—even better."

His breath feathered out in a silent laugh, and he shook his head. "Kara, even if I thought you could— You think I want a loose cannon like your father on my land?"

It was easier to attack the first half of that refusal than the second. "What do you mean, if you thought we could? Of course we could. Dad built the last one. And you won't find anybody in the state that could do it better than him—or even do it at all. Nobody builds post and beam down in this part of the country. It's almost a lost art.''

"For good reason, Kara. It's a wonderful style of architecture, but you can't find timbers big enough to do it anymore. Not in this part of the world. And it's labor intensive—it takes a big crew to frame it up.''

And they had no crew at all. But she'd worry about that later. "We'll find the wood. And we can do it. *Please*.''

He shook his head regretfully. "Not a chance.''

She could feel her own pulse where he held her, slamming against his fingers, as if her blood itself was fighting to escape that warm manacle. Dad in jail... He would die there, without her to cheer him up and take care of him. "But there's no other way we can... If you won't let us pay you back like that...''

But she might as well have pleaded with a stone. "I'm sorry, Kara,'' he said simply. "He's got to face reality some day.''

Shaking her head numbly, she looked away from those pitiless eyes to stare around the room. In one corner stood a desk, and on it was a lamp with a stained-glass shade that even she could recognize as a Tiffany. It had probably cost more than her father had earned in his whole life. This man knew *nothing* about reality and its merciless requirements.

Stonehall was still talking. "And it might do you some good, too, Kara, if he spent a few years drying out at the expense of the county. You can't spend your whole life playing nursemaid to an aging drunk.''

She'd had enough. More than she could stomach of this stone-hearted man. In spite of his hold on her she stood up abruptly.

"Where are you off to?'' he asked, looking up at her.

"Away from you,'' she said frankly.

One corner of his mouth curled ever so slowly to make an expression of irony more than amusement. "I see." He looked at the slender wrist he still held. "Well..." He brought it swiftly to his face.

Lips parting with the total shock of this, Kara watched, then felt warm lips move against the palm of her hand. A wave of heat roared up her arm and over her body, as the flames had overwhelmed the barn last night. How *dared* he, after all he'd done?

Before she could snatch her hand away, he'd set her free, leaving her skin tingling where his fingers had touched her. "God speed," he said quietly. It was a dismissal. He leaned back in his chair and closed his eyes. His chest moved in an inaudible sigh.

For a stunned moment Kara could only stand staring down at him. Odd to hate him so now, when last night she'd felt as if— She tore that thought out by the roots and whirled away from him. Hank in jail—that was what she should be thinking about. How could anyone be so heartless, so unfeeling as to put someone like her father in jail?

She started for the exit, then swerved toward the French doors. She was in no mood to meet that housekeeper again. She had her hand on the doorjamb, when the thought hit. As though struck by lightning she stood there, staring blindly at a smooth slope of hillside and the four deer that grazed just beyond the verandah.

"Yes?" Stonehall said quietly behind her.

Slowly she turned to find he'd risen from his chair and was facing her across the room. "You said a man always pays his debts?"

His brows twitched, but he nodded gravely.

Her eyes swept over him, remembering the feel of his chest under her sliding fingers, the warmth and slippery hardness of him. "Last night I saved your life, Jordan Stonehall. How do you plan to repay that?"

She didn't wait for an answer, she was too full of contempt and anger and something else entirely to stand still. She whirled out onto the verandah, stampeding the deer into snorting flight with her arrival.

"Kara, come back here!"

She was taking no orders from this brute. She was almost glad they could not agree—at least she wouldn't have to see him again! A hedge of rambler roses higher than her head blocked the way to the truck. She stopped, found the gap in it to her right and discovered that a garden gate blocked it. The gate's catch was stiff, as if no one ever came this way. As she jiggled it frantically, his hand closed on her shoulder.

"Whoa." He pulled her around to face him. "What are you talking about?"

For an instant she felt as if it were ten years ago, and she'd never grown. But it was only that he'd pulled her so close she had to tilt her head back to see his face. She was shivering all over with rage, and she gulped a deep, steadying breath, then wished she hadn't. With the inhalation, she breathed in his scent, a musky, masculine smell of leather, and sun-dried grass, with a hint of fresh sage.

"What are you talking about, saving my life?" he repeated. His fingers moved slightly on her arm, as if of their own accord.

"Joe crunched you by the door of the barn," she told him tautly. "You fell just inside the door. How do you think you got outside?"

His eyes narrowed, and he pulled her even closer, as if to get a better look. "I guess I thought—" He frowned, and his eyes dropped from hers to scan the rest of her face slowly, then came back to meet her defiant gaze. "*You* pulled me out of there half-pint?"

"I *told* you, don't call me—" She put a hand to his chest to shove him away, then hesitated, as her palm touched the bandage. She might hurt him, and furious as she was, she couldn't do that.

His eyes gleamed with laughter, but his heart was suddenly pounding beneath her palm. "You were objecting to shortstuff, I believe."

"I'm objecting to your calling me anything at all!" She yanked the arm he held backward, but he didn't let go. He simply rocked forward as she pulled, and suddenly, all that held their bodies apart was her hand on his chest. The rhythm of his breathing confused hers—his was faster, and her lungs wanted to fall in with it, even as she tried to hold her breath. She could feel his body heat washing over her. Her eyes widened.

"How am I supposed to thank you, if I can't call you anything?" he asked, and his low voice was husky with laughter.

"I—" Oh, it was so hard to speak, hard even to think with him standing so near. "I don't want your thanks. I wouldn't take it on a platter. I want repayment."

He lifted his injured arm for the first time. Its fingers moved stiffly as he captured a lock of hair at her temple. "What kind of repayment will you take, Kara Tate?" He drew the curl out to the side, then ran its sun-silvered length through his fingers, pulling ever so gently as he did so.

She wanted to close her eyes to savor the sensation, it seemed to tug at so many parts of her besides her scalp. Wanted to move her hand over his chest in slow delicious circles. This was madness. This man was the enemy. He'd lock her father in jail and throw away the key without thinking twice. And yet... She forced the soft, breathless note out of her voice. "I want Dad out of jail. And I want you to let us rebuild that barn."

He let her go and stepped back. "I'm not sure my life's worth *that* much!" His voice was a rueful growl.

"I doubt it," she agreed. "But you owe me."

He swore under his breath. "I may owe you, but I owe your dad nothing, Kara. He owes *me*, dammit!"

"That's where the barn comes in," she assured him. She was careful to keep the triumph out of her voice, but it was trembling inside her. She had him! Sheerly by accident she'd stumbled onto the one chink in his armor. That macho Stonehall pride would never let him deny a debt. And she would never let him forget he owed one, until Hank was out of danger. "Well, do we have a deal?" she pressed jubilantly.

He shook his head.

Her spirits plummeted. She'd been so sure....

"Not yet, we don't," he growled. "Does your dad know anything about this crack-brained proposal?"

He hadn't a clue, but if she told Stonehall that, the deal would be off, she was certain. "Yes, of course he does," she said, crossing her fingers behind her.

Stonehall swore again and half turned away from her, then swung back. "Let's take it one step at a time then, shall we?"

"Meaning?"

"I'll call the sheriff and have him released—though mind you that doesn't mean I can't have him re-arrested in a minute. But before I agree to let your dad build me a barn, he's going to have some conditions to meet."

"What are they?" Anything, absolutely anything at all.

"I'll have to think about that," he said darkly. "But we'll start with apologies."

"Apologies?" The dust devil churned in her stomach again. Persuade her father to apologize to a Stonehall? That would be infinitely harder than persuading him to build the barn.

Stonehall nodded. "For my barn. For all the times he's called me and my father cheats in public."

Kara gulped.

Stonehall nodded grimly. "And for a dozen other petty harassments, whenever the moon was full and he took the notion. He used to drive my father's blood pressure right through the roof. I swear if Tate had been my age I'd have whipped him within an inch of his life years ago, Kara. I'm sick of this! This time by God he learns a lesson, one way or the other."

But not the way Stonehall wanted. Not by locking him away till the last of his spirit was broken. "You'll have that apology," she told him stiffly.

"Good." He stepped close again, too close. She backed away and found herself at the gate. "No later than noon," he warned her softly. His hand moved to the gate, hemming her in.

No later than noon. He was giving the orders already. And she had a feeling that if he did agree to let them build the barn, he'd be laying down the law every last step of the way. She was going to hate this almost as much as her father. Hate it as much as she hated the way she couldn't breath when Jordan Stonehall crowded her. "By noon," she agreed breathlessly as he leaned even closer.

His mouth was so close, it filled her field of vision when he smiled. It was a lazy smile, ironic, smugly masculine.

"Good," he drawled, and his breath caressed her lips. "And he comes to see me *alone*, shortstuff. Man to man."

Mesmerized by his nearness, her breathing coming in exactly the same deep, ragged rhythm as his, she nodded, then started at the metallic snap beside her. She glanced down. He'd unlatched the gate for her. It swung out and away, setting her free.

Ears burning, she whirled and retreated into the dusk. Behind her, his soft laughter was the final humiliation.

CHAPTER THREE

HANK TATE was not a man easily angered. So this was guilt talking this morning, Kara decided. Guilt and a black depression.

And there was something else she couldn't quite name. His bluster was meant to cover something—a sense of bewildered defeat that was totally unlike his normal stubborn optimism. He had to snap out of this!

"Apologize! I'd sooner eat a tarantula than apologize to that cheating, *sneaking*—"

"Would you rather go to jail?" she cut in briskly. "That's your only choice, you know." She put the iron down and turned his only dress shirt on the ironing board. If he was going to talk to Jordan Stonehall—and that remained a very big if!—then she was determined he'd look his most respectable when he did so.

In the pocket kitchen across the motel room, Hank's muttering was drowned out by running water as he rinsed the breakfast dishes. It became audible again when he shut the water off. "...could always cut and run to California. Seems like the whole county is moving out there. I hear houses sell for an arm and two legs in L.A. If we could get somebody to back us, build a house or two on spec—"

Kara shook her head irritably and nosed the iron along the shirt's placket while steam rose around her face. Hank might be a dreamer, but he wasn't one to cut and run from his responsibilities. This was just talk, that's all it was. He wasn't going anywhere—she ought to know.

She had begged him hundreds of times to quit this town and move with her to someplace where a person could still earn a living. Because with the oil bust Texas was seeing the hardest times it had seen since the Great Depression. She and Hank had barely scraped by for the past four years. But she'd never been able to budge him. He'd listen to the glowing pictures she'd paint of how life could be someplace else—he'd even go her one better, with his dreams of becoming this or speculating in that.

But when push came to shove, he didn't want to go anywhere. It was almost as if he were nailed by his shirttails to the dry, rocky soil of this town where he'd suffered so many defeats. Is it because Mom died here? she wondered for the thousandth time. Or maybe because this was where he'd had the best years of his life with her, before she died? Whatever— "You aren't running anywhere," she told him as he turned away from the sink. "And you're the one who taught me to always be honest. We owe that man a barn."

"Yeah . . ." he admitted heavily. "Yeah, we do— *I* do." Shoulders slumped, he stood staring into space as he dried his hands. Then he shook his head with renewed energy. "But *damned* if I owe him an apology! If his dad hadn't paid me in the first place with a colt with a weak eye, none of this would have happened! That damned bad-luck barn . . ."

"If old man Stonehall did give you a horse with a weak eye, it's about time to forget it," Kara said quietly. "The man's been dead four years. It's his son who owned that barn. And it's his son who wants an apology."

"Well damned if he'll get one either! For all I know, he did something to Joe's eye that day we left him alone in the stall with him. Remember? He sure wanted to buy him back bad enough."

"Not enough to blind him in one eye!" Kara cried. "You don't believe that, Dad! And you can't have it both ways, can you?"

"I can't have it any ways," Hank muttered. "I'm blinder than ol' Joe. *I'm* the blind fool who took ten thousand for a ten-million-dollar stud." He mustered a shaky smile, but it wavered and vanished. "If I'd *just* hung on to Joe... We'd be rich by now, Kara."

"Riches don't mean that much."

"When I think of what your mother would say, seeing you living in a cockroach palace like this... I promised her I'd take care of you. See you got an education..."

Kara came to him and caught his arms. She stared into his faded hazel eyes, hardly having to tip back her head to do so. She'd inherited her small size from him, as well as from her mother. "Dad, don't start! We've been over this time and again, and you *know* I'm happy working with you." Well, maybe happy was too strong a word, but an education wasn't everything. Family mattered more. "But that's not the point, the point is we have to keep you out of jail. You *have* to apologize." She shook him gently. "And you are sorry you burned down that beautiful barn, aren't you?"

His thick, sandy lashes, which she'd also inherited, blinked rapidly. She let him go, and he shambled back to the sink to stand there staring down at it, avoiding her eyes.

"It was a beautiful barn," she insisted. "A work of art."

He reached for the sponge and wiped out the sink, then kept on wiping.

"The world's a poorer place for not having your barn in it," she said coaxingly. "Jordan Stonehall doesn't even come into this. You said it yourself, remember? That barn was the best thing you ever built."

He dropped the sponge and simply held onto the edge of the sink.

"You need to put that barn back in the world for *you*, Daddy! Apologies be darned. Apologies are just something you have to do on the way to rebuilding that barn, like choosing the wood, or buying the nails, or—"

He shook his head. "I can't, Kara."

"You've got to!" Desperately, she played her ace. "You promised Mom you'd take care of me. Is going to jail taking care of me? How long is Tate Remodeling going to survive without you? You'll be okay—you'll be eating high on the hog, care of the county, but what about me?" She smiled as he turned, to show him she was teasing, but her eyes glistened with tears.

"I can't, Kara," he repeated miserably. "I just can't go out there."

"You can! I'll go with you. It won't be that hard." As the words escaped her, she remembered a set of cold, mocking eyes, and Stonehall's warning. He wanted Hank to meet him alone. Man to man. But Hank was going to need every ounce of courage she could lend him to see him through this ordeal.

"I can't, Kara." Hank squeezed around the ironing board to his bed and sat down heavily. "It's not just the apology, it's the building. I can't do it."

"What do you mean, you can't?" She came to sit shoulder to shoulder with him. "It should be easier the second time."

Elbows on knees, he propped his face in his hands and stared at the cracked linoleum underfoot. "I didn't think I could do it the first time, even. It's not like you can buy a set of plans for a post and beam barn. It's all word of mouth.

Passed down. I had to really scramble, trying to figure out
how to do it. I'd helped my dad build a small one back when
I was a kid. But building a big one from scratch!" He
laughed mournfully. "I don't know how I did it, Kara, I
swear I don't. It was almost like that barn *wanted* to be
built. Like the timbers almost stood up and marched into
place. It was magic."

He laughed again, a rusty, hurting sound. "Boy, I
thought I was on top of the world, the day I finished that
barn! If I could do that, I figured I could do anything. There
I was, with a pretty wife and a daughter any man would be
proud of, and my very own race horse. Man, I figured we
were going places!" He laughed with that same dreary irony.

And he's never felt that way again, Kara realized with a
rush of pity. That had been the very pinnacle of his life. She
put an arm around his shoulders. "We can do it," she said
softly. "I'll help you figure out how to build it, if you've
forgotten how."

"It's more than that, Kara. I've lost my skills. Laying linoleum and installing kitchen cabinets, plastering walls,
patching roofs, that's nothing to building a big barn! It's
been ten years. I don't remember how."

"It'll come back to you," she insisted. It would have to.

"And we don't have the manpower, baby. You saw the
size of those beams in the loft, the other night. I raised that
barn with a crew of six. There's no way two runts like you
and me could do it alone."

"There is! I'm sure there is. Or if there isn't, we'll hire
help when we need it. That's what we can do."

"And we'll pay the help with what?" he asked, but at
least he sat up straight and turned to look at her.

"Why, with— With—" They'd have exactly two hundred
and eleven dollars in the bank once she settled their hospital bill. That wasn't even enough to pay for this room and

her own, anymore. "With the truck!" she said suddenly. "When we get to the point where we have to have labor, we'll sell the truck."

"If we do that, how will we get back and forth from town? And what are we going to live on, while we're building for free? And where?"

She bounced to her feet, brushing those objections aside. "You'll have to tell Stonehall that we need to live on site, so we don't lose time driving back and forth. He's got miles of land, I reckon he can spare us a little room down by his creek. We can get a tent, camp out."

Hank smiled at her excitement, but he shook his head. "It's not that simple, Kara."

He was right, but she'd never admit it. The only simple thing right now was his choice—jail or build the barn. Somehow. "We can do it!" she insisted and spun back to the ironing board. They should get going soon. There was no use riling Stonehall by missing his deadline.

Steam curling the wisps of hair upon her cheeks, she searched out the last few wrinkles around the shirt collar with the point of her iron. Hank was still brooding on the bed. Funny how he could dream—sometimes it seemed that was all he did nowadays—and yet he couldn't dream that they could do this. It was almost as if he'd burned up his best dreams with his barn. She put the iron down. Well, she'd just have to dream big enough for both of them.

"YOU CAN let me out here, Dad." Kara nodded at the stone bridge that arched over the creek. It would be cool down by the water, and it was far enough from Stonehall's house that he wouldn't see her. Or vice versa, which suited her well enough. She turned to smile encouragingly at Hank as he brought the pickup to a stop. "Are you all right?"

He didn't look all right. He looked pale and sweaty and as nervous as a chipmunk in a rattler's den. Even his bald head seemed to be sweating. Maybe she shouldn't have made him wear that tie. He hooked a finger to pull it away from his throat as if he were strangling, and nodded grimly.

"Just keep it short and simple," she advised him for the umpteenth time. "Just say you're really sorry, and we'd sure like to rebuild his barn."

The rest was up to Jordan Stonehall. She clenched her hands. How hard was he going to be on Hank? She didn't doubt for a second that he was a hard man, but was he a cruel one? She felt a shiver of cold rage trickle down her backbone. That she even had to worry about this—it was *horrible* to be so completely in a stranger's power. He could trample the last of Hank's pride and self confidence into the dust, if he felt like it. If there were only some way that she could be there to make sure he didn't! "Guess you'd better get on up there." She slammed shut the pickup's door, then gave him her warmest smile. "Go get him, tiger!"

The pickup crept up the hill toward the ranch house at a pace she could have equaled on foot. Hands in the pockets of her denim skirt, Kara watched it go, then sighed and turned to the creek.

It was a soothing sight for a worried heart. Less than ten yards wide, the creek was shaded on the far side by the giant live oaks that overhung it. The bank on this side was cleared to rough pasture that sloped up toward the distant ranch house. A faint two-wheeled track followed its winding course, then vanished around the base of the slope.

She glanced up the hill at the stone house. If Hank and she were to camp here, they would be visible from the house and the road— Stonehall wouldn't like that any more than she would. But if she followed the creek around the bend, maybe there'd be a spot where they could camp safely out of sight and mind.

Around the bend, the creek widened into a pool. It looked like a perfect swimming hole. To confirm her fancy, a thick, weathered rope dangled from an overhanging branch to trace a pale line in the dark, drifting water. She sighed with envy. What heaven it would be to come down here in the late afternoon after a hard day's work to wash your cares and your sweat away with a romp in this pool. Did Stonehall ever indulge himself so, or did he count himself too mature for such horseplay?

Forget him, she told herself irritably. An outcropping of water-smoothed limestone formed a perfect sunning shelf above the creek. Kicking off her shoes, Kara sat on the rock and dangled her feet. She let out a blissful sigh. It was a hot day for April, but even here where the sun warmed it, the water was deliciously cool. She swished her feet back and forth, admiring the topaz color of the water as it flowed across her skin.

"Darned if it ain't a Texas mermaid!" Delivered in a twangy tenor, that declaration startled her so she almost fell off her rock.

Kara swung around to find a young man grinning down at her from the back of a sorrel Appaloosa. With her sudden movement, the horse shied, snorting its surprise. Its rider swayed gracefully in the saddle and went with the mare's sidestep without seeming to be aware of it. He was too busy giving Kara an approving inspection. "I know you!" he added, when she didn't speak. "You're the gal we took to the hospital the other morning, along with the boss and that little bald guy."

"Yes." Kara recognized him now. She'd been too dazed that night to give any of Stonehall's men more than the briefest explanation or notice. At any other time, she'd have noticed this young man. He had a nice set of shoulders and, in sharp contrast to his suntanned face, the whitest, friendliest grin she'd ever seen.

"I know the boss made out okay. How about you and the other guy?" he asked now as he slacked his reins. Satisfied that Kara was not a danger, the mare dropped her head to crop the dry grass in nervous snatches.

"Nothing to speak of," she assured him. "Dad swallowed some smoke, but he's fine now."

"And you sure look fine," the young man declared, his eyes crinkling. "Doesn't take no doctor to tell that."

Kara smiled. A month ago, even a couple of days ago, she would have thought he looked pretty fine, too. With his sun-bleached hair and that wide grin, he was easy on the eyes, with a nice, easy manner. Too easy, she thought suddenly. Too young, too unsubtle. But that was odd, to be comparing him unfavorably to a man she almost hated.

The ranch hand crossed his big wrists on his saddle horn. "My name's Chris Haley. You wouldn't happen to have a name, would you?"

"Reckon I might," she told him, smiling back and then introducing herself. There was one thing to be said for such light flirtations—it was nice to feel in control, to know all the moves in the dance. And that was a far cry from the way Jordan Stonehall had made her feel yesterday.

Chris had been drawling on while her mind wandered. She looked up to find him mid question. " . . . happen to know any truth 'bout this rumor going 'round, that somebody burned that ol' barn down on purpose?"

Kara met his eyes squarely. If she was going to work around here for the next month or so, she'd better nip these rumors in the bud. "It was an accident, Chris. Truly."

Noting the determined angle of her chin, he nodded and let it go.

And now it was her turn to offer a subject change. "You know what I've been wondering though?" She'd meant to ask Stonehall yesterday, and then had forgotten it in the heat of their confrontation. "What happened to Smoky Joe? Is he all right?"

Chris laughed and leaned down to pat his mare's glossy shoulder. "You want to know that, you ought to ask this little lady here. I guess Daisy knows better than anybody."

"You don't mean—" When he grinned and nodded, Kara laughed aloud.

"Trust that ol' stud to find the closest willing lady, come hell or barn burning," he chuckled. "We had a heck of a time persuading him to say goodbye, once we caught up with them."

Kara stood, slipped on her shoes and walked over to the mare. "But she's not a Thoroughbred, is she?"

Chris laughed. "Course not. Daisy's a working gal. Joe broke into the home pasture, where I keep her nights. But the best part of the joke is, she's mine!"

Kara gave a long, appreciative whistle. She didn't know what Stonehall charged for Joe's stud fee, but it would be more than any cowboy could ever hope to afford. And Chris had gotten his mare romanced for free, since there was no way Stonehall could charge him for the unsolicited event. Meeting his dancing eyes, she laughed again. One nice thing had come of that awful night, anyway. "Maybe I *should* claim I burned down that barn!"

Daisy's head jerked up from the grass. Kara jumped backward and Chris hurriedly gathered in the mare's reins as she spun to face the approaching horse and rider.

"I don't think I'd do that," Jordan Stonehall said silkily. Halting his mount beside the Appaloosa, he stared down at Kara. "Someone might take you seriously."

Kara opened her mouth, then shut it again when nothing came out. She could feel her face flushing scarlet—even the top of her head felt hot. Funny how his eyes could look so cold, and yet she could almost smell the fire and brimstone whenever she was around him. But he made a handsome devil, she had to admit, as Stonehall turned his cutting gaze on poor Chris. He wore a pair of worn twill trousers today and a thin cotton shirt with one sleeve slit to accommodate his cast. The blue of its fabric turned his eyes to arctic ice. Stiff as he must have been from his injuries, he sat his big blood bay gelding like a Comanche.

"What are you doing here, Haley?"

Chris's lazy slouch in the saddle straightened to almost military attention. "Mike sent me to move the yearlings," he explained quickly. "I'm heading back for lunch now."

"And you'll be late if you don't make tracks," Stonehall informed him.

The younger man nodded, touched a finger to his hat-brim to Kara and reined the mare. Daisy whirled neatly and settled into a businesslike lope. They vanished around the track toward the road.

Meanwhile Kara had found her voice. "You know I was joking," she said with more assurance than she felt.

Beneath the brim of his Stetson hat, his eyes were shadowed and unsmiling. "Do I?"

She was not going to let him scare her—or at least not let him see how he scared her. "You do," she insisted. His gelding extended his nose to her, and she put a palm to its breathy softness without dropping her defiant gaze from its rider.

"And what the blue blazes are you doing here anyway?" he growled. "I told you to send your father alone."

"He is alone, Mr. Stonehall." Kara looked at her watch pointedly. "He's been up there, alone, waiting for you for over half an hour now." And had Stonehall kept poor Hank waiting and sweating on purpose? If he had, then the man was despicable.

But far from looking repentant, Stonehall shook his head in disgust. "Do you have to hold his hand every step of the way, Kara, or are you just too bossy to let him stand on his own two feet?"

"And have you stopped beating your wife yet?" she snapped back. Did he think that because she was so much younger than he, she was stupid, to try a no-win question like that on her?

His eyes crinkled suddenly, though his mouth held its carved, level line. "I'm afraid I've been neglecting that duty, since the divorce."

Her lips parted, then closed tightly. He was teasing her, wasn't he? She couldn't get a handle on him. The minute she thought she had, his mood changed. She dropped her eyes to the gelding and rubbed his red cheek. Now *his* moods she could stay on top of. The bay shook his black mane and leaned into the caress.

Divorced, was he? She seemed to remember reading something in the newspaper about an outrageously expensive wedding at the Stonehall ranch. But that would have been years ago.

And now he was divorced. That seemed strange, that a woman would leave him. In spite of his unpredictable temper and his high-handed ways, there was something about the man... Sure, she thought acidly, if you like earthquakes, and the bull ride event at the rodeo, and feeling like a fool every five minutes or so, Jordan Stonehall's your man. His ex-wife had probably run clear to Kentucky to escape that sardonic tongue and those diamond-bit eyes. She staggered as his gelding shoved his nose into her chest and nudged her enthusiastically.

Or maybe he'd left his wife. That seemed much more likely.

"If you'd stop making love to my horse," Stonehall cut into her revery, "I think it's time I spoke with your father."

Making love—? Kara found herself blushing furiously. It wasn't horses his words brought to mind, but a sudden unwelcome awareness of the lean body looming above her, and of her own heated limbs. "Yes—" She spun away to stare blindly at the creek.

He chuckled, and her hands clenched at the taunting sound. "I'd offer you a ride up to the house, shortstuff, but you're hardly dressed for it."

That jerked her head around, in spite of her blush. "I *told* you, don't call me—" But he wasn't looking at her, or not at her face, anyway. His eyes were on her sun-browned legs, revealed by her short denim skirt. Her breath caught in her throat at the expression in those eyes. The raw desire in them was totally unexpected and utterly unnerving. His teasing was hard enough to bear, but at least she knew how to respond to it. But this . . .

Those stone-gray eyes stroked the length of her, taking their own sweet time. She shivered and swung to face him, but his gaze felt no better on her heated cheeks. "I told you," she repeated helplessly, though "shortstuff" was not what she was protesting now.

"So you did, Kara Tate." His voice was husky and absent-minded, as if his thoughts had drifted far beyond her. "But you're so young . . ."

"I'm twenty!" she objected.

"And *so* short," he added mockingly, coming back into focus with an evil grin.

She threw him a smoldering look. He laughed under his breath and touched his hat, and the blood bay swung away from her.

But if he was done with her, she was not quite done with him. "Mr. Stonehall?" she called after him.

The gelding checked neatly. "Yes, Kara?"

The sun was behind him, half blinding her. She put a hand to her brow as she tipped her head back. "When you see Dad, would you remember one thing?" She paused, trying to think how to phrase it. "We may not have as much money as you, but we've got every bit as much pride." Please don't step on *his*, she wanted to beg him, but the words stuck in her throat.

She couldn't see his eyes under his hat brim, but his beautifully carved lips tightened to an unbending line. "Pride? I'd say you've got enough pride for the both of us, Kara Tate. And a bit left over." His thighs clamped together, and the bay swung around with a snort of excitement. Its rider leaned forward slightly, and the horse shot away.

The hooves of the bay seemed to echo precisely the pounding of her own heart.

CHAPTER FOUR

"THIRTY FEET," Hank Tate called from the far side of the barn's foundation.

Kara nodded, let go of the "dumb" end of the tape measure and wrote the figure down. She frowned at her notepad as she walked toward him. A thirty-foot timber, good lord, what would that weigh? For that matter, what would it cost?

"Here, honey." Hank handed her the end of the tape again, then walked the length of the foundation. As the tape spun out, Kara looked over her shoulder at their truck. They had paid three thousand for it only a week ago. But could they sell it again for that amount? She caught her lower lip with her teeth and worried it absently.

They *had* to get that much. Because that was one of the conditions Stonehall had set yesterday. His barn had been insured, but with a three-thousand deductible. That first three thousand was up to them to raise.

"Fifty feet," Hank called. Kara nodded and jotted the figure down.

Three thousand. Did Stonehall have any idea how much that was to people like them? To him, three thousand meant a weekend jaunt to Aspen or Mexico City, or a pair of custom boots. To them it meant about two months' hard labor. It meant their truck, their only transportation in this far-flung part of the world where you just couldn't get by without wheels.

Or maybe—she stumbled over a chunk of burned wood as the thought hit her—maybe he *did* realize how hard it would be for them. Maybe he'd thought the money would stop them cold. Eyes narrowed against the late afternoon sun she stood there considering, while her father walked toward her. Was that what Stonehall wanted—an excuse to escape his debt to her? An excuse to send Hank to jail? "Just try and stop us, Jordan Stonehall," she muttered aloud. "We're going to build you the best darn barn you ever saw, whether you like it or not."

Kara turned to study the Chevy truck again. If they used the truck money for timber, they wouldn't have it to spend on labor as she'd originally planned.

"Fifty feet for the plate beams...and two sills...the center beam," Hank mumbled to himself as he took the notepad from her hands. "'Course we'll piece those. Thirty-footers for the cross beams..."

A thirty-foot timber. As she imagined again what that would weigh, a feeling of cold nausea washed through her stomach. They couldn't do this—couldn't possibly do it without help. And yet they had to. Her knees felt trembly and the sun pressed down on her head like a brutal hand. She sank to the stone foundation curb, drew a shaky breath and looked at the stones on which she sat.

At least Stonehall had done them one favor. He'd ordered one of his men to clear away the remains of the old barn with the ranch bulldozer. Though come to think of it, he'd probably just despised the messiness of the burned barn. From what she'd seen of the ranch so far, he ran a tight outfit.

Whatever his motivation, the site was clear and ready to build on. That was one nasty chore out of their way. But the heavy lifting—

"You all right there, honey?" Her father looked away from his calculations to frown at her. "That sun's sure hot, isn't it? Why don't you go on back to our place? I'll be along in a little bit."

Kara shook her head. "I'm fine. Just lazy." She turned to look over her shoulder toward the foaling barn, its roof just barely peeking over the next low rise. Stonehall had given them the groom's quarters in that barn in which to live while they worked on his ranch. Not that he'd shown them the rooms himself. Mike Cavazos, the ranch foreman, had done the honors, apologizing as he did so for the spartan, but sparkling clean accommodations. Kara smiled. If Mike had seen some of the places she and Hank had lived, he wouldn't have been so quick to apologize. She'd been quite grateful that they wouldn't have to live in a tent after all.

From the corner of her eye, Kara saw something dark arching toward her. It landed near her feet—a small buffalo grasshopper. Slowly, she leaned forward over her knees to peer down at it. Black with racy stripes of red and blue, the insect crouched lower but didn't fly. Resting her chin on her crossed forearms, she studied it. Stonehall...she hadn't seen him since their meeting by the creek yesterday. Was he even on the property?

The low hum of a finely tuned engine crept into her thoughts, and she glanced aside through the sunny curtain of her hair. Speak of the devil! It was his Jaguar, approaching from the direction of the complex of barns and paddocks that sprawled out over acres and acres toward the distant river. Maybe he'd drive on by. Instead, the car stopped, and its door slammed.

She should sit up. He must want to talk to her father, and she didn't mean to let him do that without her standing by for support. Yesterday had been hard enough on Hank. But with the sun so hot, it was hard for Kara to summon her fighting spirit. Her spine seemed to have turned to melted taffy. Her nerves prickled as if a warm hand stroked her back and shoulders.

The grasshopper flung itself away as a pair of rawhide boots stopped before her. It wasn't the sun on her back she was feeling, it was Stonehall's eyes. Suppressing a shudder, Kara shoved herself upright. The movement was too sudden, and she swayed as the blood left her head.

"Where's your hat?" Jordan Stonehall demanded.

High-handed—did he think he was in charge of the whole world, or was it just everything and everyone on this ranch that he thought he owned? Well, she might be working for him, but that didn't mean he would dictate the clothes she wore. "Back in my suitcase." She hadn't had time to unpack, since their arrival this morning.

With a growl of disgust he dropped into a rider's easy crouch over his boot heels, his cast and his good arm resting on his thighs. "You're feeling faint?"

She hadn't been before his arrival. But now, with their knees almost touching... Where's Dad? she wondered with something close to panic. She wanted to look around for him but could not with Stonehall's eyes blazing out at her from the shade of his hat brim. His eyes were bright and as dangerous as the beams of a Jaguar's headlights coming right at her. She felt caught in them, the way a rabbit crouches when it should be running.

"Here." He swept off his Stetson and dropped it on her head. It fell down almost to the tip of her small nose.

And it smelled of his hair, she realized, as she sucked in her breath in surprise. A smell like new hay and sage and...and warm man. "No, thank you!" She whipped it off and thrust it back at him, her fingers tingling with the rich texture of its felt. "I don't want it."

He took it, scowled, hesitated, then said, "Too bad." He dropped it back on her head.

She reached up to yank it off again, but his hand spread on top of the crown, anchoring the hat in place. Her fingers touched his, then she snatched her hand away and sat there glowering at him from under its lowered brim. Her scalp tingled with the heavy heat of his hand, and the sensation spread in hot ripples down her nape.

Slowly he tilted the hat to a less ridiculous angle. "You have a complexion like a baby's," he told her, his mouth curling now that he'd won the dispute. "You might as well baby it."

And that's what he thought of her, wasn't it? Kara realized as she glared at him. He thought she was still a baby. It was her size, or the way he'd first met her. "I am twenty years old," she said coldly.

His grin widened. "All of that? My, my! Well, then you'd better defer to your elders, young 'un." He tapped the brim of his hat up another half inch. "Wear it till you get your own," he commanded, and stood.

Kara turned to follow his gaze and found her father hurrying from the nearest grove of oaks. "Help you?" he called to Stonehall as he came. His eyes switched to Kara with a fierce protectiveness, then to Stonehall.

Stonehall hooked his thumbs in the pockets of the faded jeans he wore and rocked back on his heels. The motion made him look even taller than he was, and Kara wondered if it was a conscious act of intimidation. He hardly needed it, the way he towered over the shorter man. Seeing Hank bristle, she felt a surge of angry sympathy.

"I'm headed for San Antonio," Stonehall said curtly. "Do you need any materials?"

Hank shook his head. He had told Kara not half an hour before that San Antonio was the first place they'd go to pick up the hardware he wanted for the job. But apparently he was accepting no aid from his enemy.

As the silence stretched thin, a muscle tightened in Stonehall's jaw. "Fine," he said, when it was apparent the other man didn't mean to speak. "I'll be back tomorrow, then." His gaze swept across Kara as he turned to go. She met it defiantly, braced against the almost tangible stroke of his eyes across her cheeks.

"And, Tate?" Stonehall swung back around. "Our agreement?"

Kara clenched her hands until her close-clipped nails bit into her palms. That had been one of the other conditions Stonehall had imposed on her father. Drink one drop of alcohol, he'd said, and the deal was off. He didn't understand at all. Didn't understand that drinking wasn't a habit with her father, but only his occasional downfall. Why, he rarely drank at all when he was working. Most galling of all, Stonehall didn't understand that once Hank Tate gave his word . . .

"I haven't forgotten," her father croaked. His hands were balled into fists like her own.

Perhaps Stonehall realized he'd gone too far in repeating that warning. But if he did, there was no way to back away from the mistake now, and he didn't try. "Good," he said quietly and left them.

Kara whipped his hat off as she rose. For a second she considered sailing it after him as he strode back to his Jaguar. "Look at me!" she wanted to call after him. "I will *not* wear your hat. I wouldn't wear your hat on a hot day in Hades!" Hat hanging down at her side, brushing her thigh, she waited for him to look back at her. But he never did.

An hour later, sitting in the office of the foaling barn with her head cocked to hold the phone receiver to her shoulder, the scene still rankled. Kara frowned at the cream-colored

Stetson hat that sat on the desk before her. And she would have to face its owner again tomorrow, to give the darn thing back, when he returned from San Antonio. She chewed her bottom lip and traced a doodle onto the blotter before her. San Antonio was no more than a two-hours' drive from here. Less, if Stonehall pushed his sleek Jaguar the way he seemed to push everything and everyone else. So why would he be staying overnight?

Unbidden, the image of his mouth floated into her mind. In spite of its habitual sternness, it was a beautiful mouth for a man. Strong and sensitive all at once.

And the way she'd caught him looking at her legs the other day—yes, there was fire smoldering under all that ice. If he ever let himself go... Was that why he was staying overnight, to let himself go with some lucky—

"Ma'am?" A man's voice spoke abruptly from the other end of the line. "Yep, we've got what you need, all right. I just measured our longest stock, and we've got thirty-footers. Prime stuff. We cut it for an architect, then he up and went broke on us."

"Great." It hadn't been easy to find timber of the length they needed, even in East Texas. This was the eighth lumber mill she'd called, and this one was way out in Big Thicket country somewhere. She talked prices for a few minutes with the mill owner, though whatever his prices, she and Hank would have to pay them. The man knew it as well as she did. After that, he gave her the directions.

"East on 190 from Livingston," she repeated, jotting it down on the blotter as she spoke. "Then south, US 92, to Fred?" She smiled at the name of the town. "Then ask anybody for Smitty's Lumber? Fine, yes sir, I reckon we can find that." She hung up as Hank stepped into the office. "I've found it!" she said triumphantly, then told him where.

"Good." Hank rubbed his shiny head. "If we leave right away, we can still make Carter's in San Antone, before they close."

"We're leaving today?" And why should that bother her? It was not as if they had to ask permission.

"Sooner we buy what we need, the sooner we finish this job." Hank gave her a little push toward the door. "You go get packed. I'm going to call your Uncle Dennis and see if they can't put us up for the night."

Kara nodded. A stop in Houston would break up the ten-hour drive nicely, and they wouldn't have to pay for a motel the first night. And she counted herself lucky if she got to see her mother's brother and his family more than once every year or two. Still . . . She glanced back at the hat. This trip should be fun. So why was she reluctant to leave?

No reason, she told herself firmly. Snatching up the Stetson, she hurried out of the office. She hadn't unpacked yet and neither had Hank, so packing would be a snap. They could just grab their suitcases and go.

THAT HAT'S haunting me, Kara decided the next afternoon as she shut the door to her motel room behind her. Stonehall's Stetson hat had purposely followed her half the long way across Texas, it almost seemed. And now, sitting there on her bed where she had tossed it when she checked into this motel near Fred a few hours ago, the cowboy hat looked almost smug.

Yesterday she had brought it along in the truck, meaning to drop it off at the big house on their way off the ranch grounds. That had seemed the smart thing to do. But she and Hank had got to talking. First thing she'd known, she'd been halfway to San Antonio with the darn thing sitting on the seat beside her.

As Kara unbuttoned her shirt, then slid out of her jeans, she scowled at the Stetson. She could almost believe it was watching her. How could she be embarrassed by a darn hat? "Hah!" she told it contemptuously, and tossed her brassierre across it.

But that hat was shameless. It looked quite at home on her bed, cuddled up with her lingerie. Nose high, she stalked past it and into the bathroom. Hank had stayed at the lumber mill to help the men choose and cut a couple of tall trees to be gin poles, whatever those might be. And then he was going to help them load the big lumber truck that would carry the makings of the barn to the ranch tomorrow morning.

So she had all the time in the world for a shower and maybe a cat nap. Smitty, the owner of the mill, had promised to drop Hank off this evening on his way home from the lumberyard. He was being wonderfully helpful, which made Kara suspect that they had not struck such a good bargain in trading their pickup for his timber. Oh, well, the deal was made now. Tomorrow she and her father would turn over the keys to the Chevy pickup, then ride back to Kerrville in the lumber truck.

When she'd finished a long, refreshing shower, Kara wrapped herself in her terry cloth robe. Combing her hair out, she wandered restlessly around the shabby room. She didn't feel like having a nap after all. She needed to . . . She wanted to . . . She didn't know what she wanted. Only that it was not here, whatever it was. "Let me know, when you figure it out," she growled aloud, then jumped as someone rapped sharply on her door.

That would be Hank, of course. "That didn't take so long," she remarked cheerfully as she opened the door.

The steel-gray eyes of Jordan Stonehall drilled into her.

"Eep!" she yelped and tried to slam the door shut. But his boot jammed into the crack. As she retreated, the door rebounded and swung wide. "What are you—? How did you—?" Her voice stuttered to a halt.

She had wondered what he'd look like if he ever let himself go. Well, she was a little closer to knowing. But blazing mad as he was, he still walked the razor's edge of control. He stepped into the room in one tiger-smooth stride and shut the door behind him. His eyes raked her from head to bare toes and his mouth curled in disgust.

Who was he to look at her that way, as if he saw her stripped naked and didn't care for the view? Even as she flinched under those whiplash eyes and hugged herself, her chin lifted defiantly.

"You lovely little liar!" he growled. He took a step toward her, but when she backed away from him, her eyes widening, he stopped. At his sides his hands moved restlessly, his fingers extending as if they longed to reach out and grab her, to shake her within an inch of her life.

"Wh-what— What are you talking about?" she stammered.

"At my age I should know—if it looks too good to be true, then it is." His eyes swept over her face and damp curling hair, and when he moved forward this time, it was with the smooth inevitability of a wave rising toward the shore.

There was nowhere to escape him in this tiny room. And instinctively she knew that to try would be the worst mistake of all. Heart pounding, she tipped her chin to meet those merciless eyes. He seemed to hang above her like a wall of cold, gray water about to come crashing down.

His left hand raked into her hair, closed on it and tugged her head back. The action swayed her forward. Gasping, she put a hand to his chest, holding him off. Beneath her palm he was hot as a stove, his heart slamming against her. That was more frightening than anything, that he could look so icily deliberate, while all that battering fury was walled within. She shivered and tried to shake her head, but his fingers tightened in her hair. "Wh-what are you talking about?" she repeated desperately.

"Cut the innocent act! You con me into letting your bum of a father out of jail, then the first chance you get, the two of you hightail it. That's what I'm talking about!"

That's what he thought? She felt a rush of bewildered relief—this was all a mistake!—then a rapidly kindling rage. They had given their word, after all! Did he think that meant nothing? She pushed hard on his chest, feeling the tape under his shirt, but instead of letting her go, he caught her waist with his good hand. Hard fingers bit into her through the terry cloth.

It was difficult for her to think, facing the fury in his eyes. More difficult to know what to say, as his thumb stroked a slow, insolent arc up the soft curve of her stomach, then down again. "I didn't lie to you," she insisted shakily.

"No?" His voice had roughened, but it held something more than anger now. "You promised me a barn, Kara Tate." His thumb traced its curving path again, pressing the soft texture of the terry cloth into her flesh, while the fingertips at the back of her waist tightened. "Next thing I know, you've packed your bags and gone. One thing you'd better learn and learn fast, girl, is that nobody makes a fool of me."

"Who needs to, when you make such a good fool of yourself?" she cried. "What do you think we're doing here, Dad and me, anyway? Or did you think at all?"

His head jerked back with her counterattack, and those dark, level brows drew together dangerously. But then he blinked, as if her words were just now hitting home. "I thought . . ." His eyes narrowed and swept over her flushed face. "I assumed you had folks here that you'd run to. Or possibly you'd found a job."

As he spoke, his thumb retraced its restless path. The caress was seductive, maddening—she couldn't breathe right while he did it. Catching his thumb with her free hand, she curled her fingers tightly around it. She could feel his blood hammering in the wide base of it. "You *didn't* think!" she snapped. "You jumped to conclusions. And my father is *not* a bum. Now take your hands off me before I scream this place down!"

Miraculously his hands dropped away. She glared at him, found that the corners of his mouth were beginning to twitch, then looked to where her fingers still clamped around his thumb. She dropped it like a hot potato, and whirled away from him.

"All right, I'll ask," he growled as she stalked away from him. "What *are* you doing here?"

She reached the far wall and swung to face him. "We came to buy wood. For your barn."

His brows jerked slightly. "With what?"

His surprise was almost the biggest insult of all. Not only did he think of them as bums, he thought they were paupers! Well, that might be close to the truth, but anyone with an ounce of manners— Eyes flashing, she paced toward him. "That's none of your business, where we get our money! We owe you three thousand, we're paying you. That's all that concerns you."

He didn't like that—his face hardened, but she didn't care what he liked anymore. She paced three steps along the wall.

"Where's your dad?" he asked, addressing her rigid back.

She shot him a smoldering look over her shoulder. "At the mill, helping load the delivery truck." And now it was her turn to ask something. She swung around and prowled toward him. "How did you find us?"

"It wasn't hard. You scribbled a few notes on the blotter by the phone." He returned her frown. "You could have saved me a heap of trouble by simply leaving me a message before you took off like that!"

"*Mr.* Stonehall, we are contractors, not indentured servants. We'll build you your barn, but we'll come and go as we please while we're doing it." Though there would be a lot less coming and going once their truck was gone, she admitted to herself ruefully.

"I see," he said, neither accepting nor contesting that. His lips twitched again. Hooking his hands in the snug Levi's jeans he was wearing today, he rocked on his boot heels, then swung around idly, surveying her room. But as his gaze swept across the bed, his whole body froze.

Kara's eyes followed his, and she found herself staring at his hat on the bed. Her lacy, peach-colored bra still encircled it in a lewd embrace. *"Umm!"* she murmured mindlessly, her brain in neutral and revving out of control. A red-hot tidal wave was rushing up her skin from somewhere around her waist. She glanced in helpless outrage at her companion, as if somehow he were responsible for the ridiculous tableau.

Stonehall's tanned face was split in a grin of sheer bliss. He turned to her, saw the look on her face—his head tipped back in a roar of delighted laughter.

Pouncing on the obscene duo, she snatched her bra away and hurled it at her open suitcase. She crossed her arms tight and glared at the far wall, the ceiling—at anything and everything but him. Taking in deep gulps of air to try to cool her face, she waited for Stonehall to stop hooting.

"I like your hatband!" he chortled once he caught his breath.

She hunched her shoulders and glared at the far corner. Couldn't he see she wanted to be alone? If he had a shred of decency he'd leave now.

Instead he crossed to her suitcase. Her lips parted in protest. If he touched her brassierre, she would—

She wasn't sure what she'd do, but sure as shooting, it would not be legal.

But he didn't molest her lingerie. Instead he chose a neatly folded shirt, and after a moment's hesitation a pair of her white painter's pants. Turning, he held them out to her. "Get dressed," he said pleasantly.

"Why?" And what nerve he had, to think he'd tell her what to wear!

His eyes played across her bathrobe. His lips curved as he apparently chose one answer to that question, then discarded it. "Because it might get a bit drafty, traveling in that robe."

Traveling? With him, did he mean? She shook her head so hard her hair fanned out around her. "I'm not going anywhere, thanks. Dad will be back in a few hours, and he'll expect to find me here."

"He can find you at the ranch." Coming to her, he caught her hand and lifted it, then piled the clothes on the crook of her arm. "You can leave him a note, which is more than you left me."

"No." She wouldn't do it. Couldn't be cooped up in a car with this man for a full day. What would they say to each other? She shook her head.

"What's the matter, Kara?" he jeered softly. "Are you afraid?"

Was it so obvious, how much he bothered her? She shook her head angrily. "That's not it." Not entirely.

"Or is it your dad again? You don't trust him to handle buying some wood, without your holding his hand?"

She frowned, remembering what a large part she'd played in today's bargaining. She *had* been a big help. Why should she be ashamed of that? But maybe it wasn't her father Stonehall was attacking at all. Maybe he was saying that she was an overbearing, domineering little shrew? Uncertain which wrong-headed opinion of his she should be countering, she opened her mouth, then shut it again.

He patted her stack of clothes. "Get dressed. We're losing daylight."

"No."

His hand rose to the V where the sides of her robe overlapped. Catching the edge of a lapel between two fingers, he smiled down at her. "It hasn't occurred to you that I still don't know if you're lying, has it?"

Her cheeks burned again, and she couldn't have said if it was her returning anger or his outrageous intimacy that drove the blood to her face.

His fingers moved up the lapel an inch or two, then down again, the side of one finger brushing her skin with a feather touch. "For all I know, all your fine indignation is just a world-class performance. Since I'm not sure, it's easier to take a good-conduct prize."

She shook her head, more protesting what that caress was doing to her pulse than his words. She could hardly hear them at all, above the roaring in her ears.

"So go get dressed," he said huskily, "unless you want some help doing it."

He was bluffing. She was sure of that. Almost sure of that. But the image was so vivid in her mind—his hands skimming under her robe, curling around her bare shoulders, then smoothing down over her shoulder blades, brushing the robe off her body in one slow, warm caress—that she couldn't wholeheartedly disbelieve the possibility, no matter how much she wanted to.

And if she stayed here debating possibilities, he would hypnotize her with his touch and that teasing, seductive growl. Shaking her head as one awakening from a strange dream, she backed away from him toward the bathroom.

He smiled, as if that was just what he'd wanted her to do. A spark of rebellion lit within her. At least she could choose her own clothes! She spun away from his taunting eyes to stare down at her suitcase.

But there was no way she could think about fashion with his eyes warming the back of her neck. Her denim skirt was the first thing her gaze fell upon. It would work well with the yellow pinstripe oxford shirt he had chosen. She slung it over her shoulder and dropped the pants back in the suitcase. She turned to make sure he had noted her act of defiance, and surprised him in an expression of the smuggest amusement.

Startled she stared at him, then turned and fled for the bathroom.

It was only when she had locked the door behind her that the suspicion hit. That grin— Could Stonehall read her that well? Could he predict that, if he chose those pants, then just to assert her independence, she'd choose something else instead? Appalled, she stared at the skirt in her hands. Could it be that by choosing this skirt, she'd chosen precisely what he wanted her to wear? "You— Why, you polecat!" she whispered.

But here she was, stuck with the choice of a bathrobe that seemed almost more his than hers now that he'd touched it, and the blasted skirt. Gritting her teeth, she slipped out of the robe.

CHAPTER FIVE

BY THE TIME she'd dressed, Kara felt calmer. As she turned up her sleeves, she studied her reflection in the mirror. The pale yellow shirt went well with the sun streaks in her ash-blond hair and the tiny gold studs in her ears. She looked neat and in control, old enough to know her own mind. And right now her mind said she was going nowhere with Jordan Stonehall.

That decided she slung the robe over her arm, braced herself and marched out into the bedroom. But Stonehall was gone. So was his hat—and her suitcase. With a hiss of exasperation, she started for the door, then saw that he'd left her blue leather heels behind. She strapped them on, swept her hair back from her face and stalked out of the motel room.

And came face to face with Stonehall. She stopped short, and he reached around her to pull the door shut.

"Wait a minute!" she cried, a second too late. "My room key's inside."

"No, I've returned it already, and checked you out." He took her elbow and steered her toward an ancient MG convertible, with its top up, that was parked beside her truck. "I've left a message for your father at the front desk. Want to add anything to it?"

He was already opening the car door for her. Tongue-tied with irritation, she turned to the MG. He'd stored her suitcase in the compartment behind the sports car's two seats.

Well, it was coming back out of there! She knelt on the seat and reached for it, half expecting him to try to stop her, or to shut the door, closing her in. He didn't.

The suitcase was almost too big for the storage space, and it seemed to be wedged in place. She tugged at it, then the door opened beside her and Stonehall folded his long length into the low-slung car.

"I'm not going," she panted and tugged on the suitcase again.

The car's engine purred into life.

"I'm not going to be a hostage in your silly game. You can go to the mill and look at the wood yourself, if you won't believe me."

"Why don't we do that?" he agreed. Leaning past her, he slammed her door shut, his arm sliding across her hips as he reached for the door handle.

At the contact she squeaked in protest and arched away from it. The car revved smoothly and reversed in a curve across the parking lot.

"Wait!" she yelped, "I'm not going!"

"You aren't?" he asked as he pulled out onto the highway.

"No, I'm not! Stop the car."

"Too late now," was all he said as he shifted up through the gears. The little car snarled out of the town as he headed it south.

Clenching her fists, she fought the urge to turn and pummel him. "You're going the wrong way," she said coldly. "The mill's the other direction, if you mean to see it." And if he did, then that was precisely where she would get out of this car.

The corner of his mouth curled, and again she had the nasty feeling that he knew what she was thinking. "We'll eat first," he said. "It might improve your temper."

At that crack, she crossed her arms firmly over her breasts and scowled out at the endless pine trees while the little car sped south. In the town of Beaumont, he maneuvered the MG down a long, leaf-shadowed driveway and halted before a white antebellum manor. Gigantic magnolias arched overhead. Kara flashed him a look of distress. He was taking her to eat at a friend's house? She wasn't up to coping with that right now. Probably not ever—this was out of her league. "Look, your friends aren't expecting me, and I'm not hungry anyway. I'll wait in the car."

That wonderful grin of his whipped into view, just as he swung out of the car. But it was gone by the time he rounded the MG and opened her door for her. "This is a restaurant, Kara."

Feeling utterly gauche, she nodded tightly, then preceded him up the ancient brick walk to a door topped by an exquisite fanlight.

If this was a restaurant, Kara soon concluded she'd been eating in greasy spoons all her life. The maître d' conducted them through a dim interior in which silver and china and antique mahoghany furniture gave back the soft light in rich, honeyed gleams. They mounted a curving staircase, then stepped out onto a balcony where a few widely spaced tables overlooked a garden. Below their table a fountain splashed musically. Birds darted back and forth through the trees that brushed the balustrade, while a ceiling fan turned lazy circles overhead.

On the white lace tablecloth, enough silver was laid out to furnish a family picnic, but from the way the implements were grouped, Kara suspected they were all for her. Beneath the table, she clenched her hands in her lap. This was his world, and she was bound to make a fool of herself, blundering into it. Something stirred deep within her, and she wasn't sure if it was anger or pain, or only the first pangs of hunger.

But when the menus were presented, she decided it was anger.

"The shrimp *étouffée* is good," he told her.

"For that price, I hope they give you the shrimpboat as well as the shrimp!" she growled without meeting his eyes.

He laughed under his breath. "Get it and see."

Once the waiter had left with their order, she felt Stonehall settle back in his chair and turn his full concentration upon her. She studied the tablecloth. The lace dipped and swirled in patterns as intricate and confusing as those twisting inside her.

"When you pout," Stonehall said with quiet deliberation, "you look adorable. And about twelve years old."

Her eyes flashed up to find his waiting. In their gray depths she could read amusement and something darker. She would have almost guessed it was frustration, but that made no sense. *She* should be the frustrated one. "I wasn't pouting."

"No?" he challenged. "Then what were you doing?"

The waiter reappeared to place two exquisite salads before them. There were greens on the eggshell-thin plates that Kara had never seen before in her life. "I was wondering why you brought me here."

His eyebrows drew together. "Why? Because the food's good, and believe it or not, it's fast. And because the next place I know the food's worth eating is thirty miles down the road at Sabine Pass, and we don't have time for that today."

Time for that *today*. The phrase had an odd ring. For just a second she imagined having time for that with him some other day, then dismissed the absurdity. This was a once-in-a-lifetime event, and the sooner it was over, the happier she would be. It was just that he'd taken her out of her world...that's why she felt so lost.

"It's a little roadside fish-fry joint," he continued easily when she didn't speak. "With picnic tables looking out over the Gulf. And it serves the freshest fried shrimp in Texas. You get that and a bottle of ice-cold Dos Equis beer, you think you've died and gone to heaven."

Yes, that sounded more like her kind of place, but his reminiscences did little to cheer her. He was at home in both worlds, hers and his, wasn't he? Or in any world? He could sit here at ease in his worn old jeans and yet pronounce all the French names of the dishes with an accent that brought an approving nod from their snooty waiter. And somehow she knew he'd look just as at ease mending a barbed-wire fence or sitting a cutting horse while it worked a frantic calf from a herd. It wasn't fair.

He reached across to tug a lock of hair that curled upon her shoulder. "Eat, if you aren't going to talk to me. We've got to get a move on."

Kara found out what his hurry was soon after they left the restaurant. She'd been frowning at the road, trying to remember if this was the way they'd come, and beginning to fear it was not. When they skirted a small airport, she was sure of it. "This isn't the way to Fred!"

"No." He turned into the gates of the airport, then cut around to a side of the field where a number of private planes were lined up on the asphalt.

"But you said we'd look in at the lumberyard!"

"We will," he said as he parked the car in front of a long, low shed. "That is, we will if we get up before sunset."

"*Up?*" she gulped, but she was guessing already.

That brief grin of his flashed again as he swung out of the sports car, then leaned back in for her suitcase. "How'd you think I got here so fast?"

SHE WOULDN'T need an airplane to fly, Kara concluded. She had enough butterflies swarming in her stomach to float her from here to Kentucky. She peered through the plane's windshield at Stonehall and his friend in the greasy, mechanic's overalls. The two of them had been circling the twin engine plane for the past ten minutes—inspecting this, tweaking that, while she sat in the passenger seat developing a horrible case of cold feet.

How had it come to this? She'd started out to take a shower and a catnap and the next thing she knew, she'd been kidnapped, fed the most expensive meal she'd ever eaten in her whole life and was now about to depart the earth. *"Fly, I mean!"* She amended that thought hastily. Knowing Jordan Stonehall seemed to be one long, terrifying slide down the slippery slope to who-knew-what final disaster. Things had gone from bad to worse ever since he'd come into the picture.

Right now she wasn't sure what scared her more, flying for the first time in her life—and in a tiny airplane!—or the fact that she was going to be cooped up in this cramped space with Stonehall. Outside, the last rays of the sun were turning his lean face to a mask of copper, as beautiful as it was subtly menacing. The illusion shattered as he laughed at a comment from his friend. He slapped the man's shoulder and turned away.

He'd barely closed his door and settled into his seat beside her before she asked, "How long have you been flying?"

His lips twitched as he turned to the instrument panel. "Long enough." He flipped a switch, scrutinized a bank of dials, turned something else and the engines roared into life.

"How high up will we be?"

"High enough." He rotated another knob. Kara jumped as a man's voice rang out in the cabin, and Stonehall quickly turned the volume down.

"What about your cast? Won't that make it hard to steer?"

"No." Leaning over her, Stonehall caught a buckle she hadn't noticed, and pulled a shoulder harness across her.

His hands didn't touch her, and his face was impersonal as he buckled her in, but still her breath caught in her throat as the belt tugged gently between her breasts. "Wh-where do you keep the parachutes?" she babbled.

He looked at her solemnly. "Wouldn't you prefer I concentrated on flying, at least while we take off?"

"Oh—yes! I mean, *please* don't let me distract—" But he'd already gone back to his preflight sequence, with the corner of his mouth upturned ever so slightly. A few minutes later they rolled out onto the runway. The small plane was vibrating as it waited, poised for takeoff, and her teeth were chattering their own rhythm of excitement and terror.

The radio voice drawled a cheerful instruction, and Stonehall answered. Reaching out, he caught her nearest hand, which was clenched around her kneecap. "Trust me, you'll love it." Letting her go, he sent the plane rumbling down the runway.

Sun-reddened concrete streamed underneath them, the sound of the engine mounted toward a snarling crescendo, blue lights at the edge of the runway and dandelions in the field alongside rippled past and turned to streaks of running color. And then they were bounding skyward, rushing up into bright light, looking down at the darkening earth as they banked slowly above it. Kara laughed a soft, bubbling laugh of triumph and wonder, then turned to see if he felt it, too.

He did. She could see it in the glow in his eyes as he looked back at her. "Yes," he said simply.

It was the first time they'd ever been in total accord. Hanging above the earth, bathed in the red light of the sun, dancing on air, it suddenly seemed not only right that she be here with him, but inevitable, as if he were the only person in the world who could have brought her to this pinnacle of delight. She laughed again, then suddenly shy, looked away.

Below them the earth rolled in dusky splendor, huge but intricate, laced with moving lights that must be cars, spangled with yellow house lights, and splotched with lakes that mirrored the paler sky. The plane turned as it climbed, and the sinking sun lay off to their left now. "We're heading north?" she asked after a few minutes of silent enchantment.

"To stay out of Houston, and then Austin air space, as much as we can," he agreed. "We'll turn west soon."

She nodded happily, then gave a cry of delight as she pointed out a ragged cloud to the east. High enough to be still catching the sunlight, it burned like a cloth of gold.

"What did I tell you?" he said with a touch of pardonable smugness.

Overwhelmed, Kara shook her head. "Mr. Stonehall, I can't tell you how—"

"Jordan," he corrected her quickly. "If you're going to be my copilot, you'll have to call me Jordan."

Jordan. It fit him, but it didn't seem fitting for her to use it. She nodded uncertainly.

"It's not hard to pronounce," he teased when she didn't speak. "Try it."

With an inward smile she shook her head. "You're too old," she said gravely, teasing him back. He deserved it for calling her a young 'un, the other day.

His dark brows drew together sharply. "Too—just how old do you think I am?"

She knew exactly—he was thirty. "Ohhhhh...forty?" she guessed, struggling not to laugh.

"Forty!" He swore under his breath then shot her a frown as she began to giggle. His mouth curved in a reluctant grin. "Forty, my eye, you half-pint brat."

That stung—for just a second there she'd been feeling fully his equal, not half a generation his junior. "Better too short than too old," she retorted, her smile starting to fade.

"I don't know about that," he almost growled, then turned his attention back to the sky.

After a few minutes Kara realized he was following a road below.

"That's Fred down there," Jordan said, nodding at a tiny cluster of lights ahead. "The sawmill's north of town?"

"Northwest." Her stomach lurched as the plane banked to the left, and then it seemed to continue its sickening yaw. He still didn't believe her about the wood, did he? Here they'd been laughing and teasing, while all the time he still thought she might be lying. She felt as if a rug had been yanked out from under her, or rather, a flying carpet, and now she was tumbling back to the dark earth below.

"There it is."

The plane banked again, and Kara looked down on a clearing in the woods. She could just make out the stumps of logged trees, and the big shed that housed the mill itself. A long lumber truck was parked outside it, loaded and ready for its trip to Kerrville tomorrow. "There's your wood," she said tonelessly.

The plane leveled out, and now they were heading toward the last rosy glow on the horizon. Finally he spoke. "What's the matter?"

Her hands clenched tighter in her lap. "You're such a trusting sort!" she said bitterly.

"Am I?" The words were very dry.

"I'm not used to people thinking I'm a liar, or that my father is! Anyone in Kerrville will tell you we stand by our word."

His fingers drummed on the steering yoke, then his breath escaped in something between a sigh and a hiss of exasperation. "I'm *not* a trusting sort, Kara. Only fools operate from faith or from hope. I like to know the facts."

"Well, now you know the facts about us," she said.

"I'll know tomorrow," he corrected her calmly. "If and when that truck arrives at my ranch."

She bit down on her lip, the pain masking a deeper pain within. "And if it doesn't?" Trucks had breakdowns. Flat tires.

"Then I've got you instead," he said softly.

She shot him a furious glance, but he didn't return it. His lips curved in the faintest of smiles; he looked out into the dusk.

Huddling in on herself, Kara stared out her window at the blinking green light on her wing tip. How long would this miserable flight take? She didn't want to ask him, but she hoped it would not be long. Her eyes switched ahead, and now she could see the sprawling glow of a huge city to the southeast. That would be Houston—they had miles and miles to go yet. She shivered and hugged herself harder. He had come so far to catch her and her father! And he'd flown all this way on the basis of a few notes scribbled on a desk blotter and a wild hunch.

She shivered again. To go to so much trouble he must have been bound and determined they wouldn't escape him—he was more vindictive than she'd ever dreamed. Because this all came down to revenge, didn't it? He was determined to get back his own for the barn, if he had to chase them to the ends of the earth.

Kara closed her eyes, shutting out the night sky and the man by her side. Hurting all over, she concentrated on the song of the engines and tried to forget that for just a little while today, she'd started to like this man.

She woke once or twice during the flight, once when rain spattered briefly on the windshield, and once when Stonehall made a slight correction in their course. Each time, she kept her eyes nearly shut, looking into the cockpit through lowered lashes. She didn't want him to know she was awake, or to speak to her.

It was the change in the sound of the engines that woke her the next time. Her eyes drifted open, then she sat up with a start. Her seat was angled down. *"Where—?"*

"Coming down," he said calmly.

Ahead in the darkness, a string of lights appeared. The plane was aimed right at them, cutting swiftly down over the dark hills. The lights rushed up to meet them, then suddenly they were skimming over the single runway, but too high to land. The runway ended, and they went banking out over a long treeless hill.

"Just making a pass to spook any deer that might be around," Stonehall murmured. "You don't want to hit one, while you're touching down."

"No," she agreed fervently. When he straightened out the plane again, the runway lights gleamed ahead. "Who turned the lights on?"

"Hush." The command was almost soothing, the way he said it.

Kara hushed and held her breath for good measure. She didn't let it out again till the plane touched down. Then she let it out in a gasp while the plane rumbled to the end of the runway.

She continued taking deep breaths of thanksgiving while the plane taxied back toward a small shed and the Jeep parked beside it. They stopped near the shed, then he cut the engines.

After listening to their growl for so long, the silence was unnerving. "Well," Kara said, then could think of nothing to add. She couldn't say thank you for the ride, when she'd neither asked for it nor wanted it.

He seemed to be waiting for her to continue. When she didn't, he put a hand to his door. "Stay there." He stepped out of the plane.

Stay there. Hush. He spoke to her as if she were a puppy. Or a child. Gritting her teeth, she unfastened her harness and turned toward her door. She didn't want to stay here. What was the sense in that?

But her door opened from the outside, and Stonehall stood below her, hands outstretched. "Let's go."

She hesitated. Sure it was a long step down, but she was agile.

He didn't give her time to collect herself. With his typical impatience he reached in to clamp large hands about her waist.

"Wait, I can—" But he drew her out of the plane. There was nothing to do but put her hands out. Nothing for her to grip but his broad shoulders, and as she remembered his injured arm, she did her best to rest her weight on them. He set her lightly down, and their bodies were almost touching. She snatched her hands away from his shoulders, but he didn't release her.

If anything, his hands tightened, and she sucked in her breath with the sensation. Their grip made her feel possessed. Claimed.

The distant lights didn't illuminate his face so much as turn it to a stark and ruthless mask. She shivered, remem-

bering what he had said earlier: *I have you instead*. Yes, he
had her. His arms moved, swaying her toward him. She bent
like a willow, arching her neck to keep her eyes on his face.
Did he mean to kiss her? The thought sent a shaft of panic
ripping right through her. She had to say something to stop
him! "Wh-who put on the lights?" she stuttered, choosing
the first question that popped into her head.

She felt his body jerk with surprise, then slowly he smiled.
One by one his fingers loosened, as if he had to consciously
command them to straighten. "Mike had orders to turn
them on at sundown." Beneath the roughness of his voice,
amusement quivered.

"You mean we're back at your ranch?" She'd assumed
this was a private airport somewhere in the county, but not
that private.

"We're home," he agreed. His hands dropped away from
her. "Go sit in the Jeep. I'll be a few minutes, putting this
baby to bed."

This time the order did not rankle. She went gladly, knees
shaking from the closeness of the encounter. Wrapping her
arms tightly around her, she stared up at the star-struck
Texas sky. What would it be like to be kissed by Jordan
Stonehall? She knew instinctively that his lips would be
smiling that ironic, so confident smile as they took hers. She
knew how good he would smell, but there was one thing she
couldn't imagine at all. How she would feel if he ever did it.

She stirred nervously. *Stop thinking about it*. Thinking
too much about things you feared was almost a way of calling them down upon you. She jumped, then swung around
as the lights along the runway blacked out. She had forgotten her suitcase, she realized suddenly. She put a hand to the
Jeep's door, then stopped. She could trust Jordan not to
forget it.

In the physical world, she was already sure she could trust him in every way. She could trust him to fly her safely across Texas, to know the best restaurant, or the finest horse, even when it came clothed in as ungainly a package as Smoky Joe. And some instinct told her that if he was that good and sure in the physical world, he would make love to a woman with the same devastating skill. A woman could trust him with her body. But with her heart?

Stop thinking about it! she told herself savagely, as he loomed beside the Jeep. He swung her suitcase into the back seat, then slipped in beside her.

They didn't talk for a mile or more. The Jeep growled along the ranch road, raising dust behind, its headlights bumping skyward with each dip in the track. Transfixed by its lights, five deer froze in the road ahead. Stonehall tapped his horn, and they turned like dancers, then leaped the high rail fence, one after the other, like the sheep you count in dreams.

They rounded another hill, passed through an open gate guarded by a cow catcher that rumbled as the Jeep crossed over it, and still Kara did not know where they were. She looked up into the sky and found Job's Coffin, then the Big Dipper, and from there the North Star. So they were heading east.

"You're sleeping at the big house tonight," Stonehall said beside her.

"What?" she asked, unwilling to believe this new absurdity. She was too tired to cope with it. She had to get away from this man, get her feet back on the ground. Her body still felt as if it were flying—lost somewhere up in all those stars.

"You heard me." They rounded a bend in the road and the creek flowed to meet them. They were on the road she had walked a few days before.

"Yes, but— I have my own place—the groom's apartment. I want to go there."

"Not till your father returns." He shifted down as they started up the long hill to the house itself.

Till her father returned—as if she were a child in need of a baby-sitter! Or—a worse thought hit her. "What do you think, Mr. Stonehall, that I'll sneak off in the night? You're planning to lock me in a room till Dad shows up with the wood?"

He swore under his breath. "That's not why at all, Kara. And the name's Jordan. Use it."

"Then why is it, Jordan Stonehall?" she challenged him.

The Jeep had reached the crest of the hill. It jerked to a halt before the house as he jammed on the brakes. "This is why!" His hand hooked around the nape of her neck and he pulled her forward.

However she'd imagined his kiss, it had not been like this. Open-mouthed, she stared up at him, and he was not smiling at all. Then his angry face blocked out the stars, and his lips were warm and hard upon her. She gasped, and his lips stole her breath away. His heat washed over her—she put up her hands to fend him off, but instead her fingers curled into his shirtfront.

His heart was pounding under her hands, her own heart thundering in her ears. Surprise was turning to a sensation of angry hunger. How *dare* he do this to her? And now that he'd done it, how dare he stop before she'd had even a chance to comprehend the emotions roaring through her? For he was growling something into her mouth that sounded like a curse. He pushed her back against her seat and pulled away from her.

They both were panting. They glared at each other like fierce enemies, her hands still spread on his heaving chest.

"That's why," he rasped. "There are a dozen men working on this ranch, Kara, and not a one of them hasn't thought about doing that. Understand now?"

She shook her head, not denying her understanding of what he'd said, but not agreeing. She'd worked with men all her life, and he had a fine crew as far as she'd seen. She didn't feel in danger here.

He snorted incredulously. "Well if 'show and tell' didn't get the point across, I don't know what to say! It's up to your father to explain the facts of life, not me."

Show and tell—that's what he thought he'd been doing? "I understand the facts just fine, thank you!"

"Good. Then start acting like you do. Step one is to let go of my shirt."

He was despicable! It was that husky note of laughter that had crept into his voice that she hated most of all. She snatched her hands away.

He let her go more slowly, as if she were an angry cat, and he not sure if she would jump away from him or scratch his eyes when he freed her. She leaned as far away from him in her seat as possible.

"Step two is to learn to accept what you cannot change," he continued. "You're in my care until your father comes back—no ifs, ands or buts about it. That means I can sleep on the couch in your apartment, and the men will have a fine time wondering what I've been up to when they see me leave tomorrow morning. Or you can take the guest room up here, where no one's likely to cross your path."

He was herding her toward the choice he had made for her like a coyote nipping at the heels of a sheep. Frustration seethed within her, but she could see no way to vent it. She looked away from him and heaved a deep breath, then wished she hadn't. The movement of her breasts made her all the more aware of his body only inches from her own.

He caught a lock of her hair and tugged it gently. "Come on, Kara, the beds are better up here. And I'm not a cradle snatcher."

Her head snapped around. "Get this through your *thick* head, Jordan Stonehall! I...am...not...a...child!" With all the dignity that she could muster, she opened her door and slid out of the Jeep. Stalking up to the front of the stone house, head held high and proud, she left him to carry her suitcase.

CHAPTER SIX

"You like more *café*?" asked Jordan Stonehall's housekeeper as she crossed the upstairs deck to the table where Kara sat.

Kara smiled, touched the sterling silver coffeepot that sat on the tray before her and shook her head. "No, thank you, Mrs. Cavazos. I've drunk too much already. I should get up and get moving." But she was reluctant to leave. It was so beautiful up here on the deck built above the kitchen wing.

A rough-beamed arbor had been built over half the deck. Grape vines and red honeysuckle filtered out the worst of the Texas sun. Beneath it, delicate patterns of sunlight and shadow played across the red floor tiles and her table each time the warm breeze blew. The scent of honeysuckle was so strong it seemed to flavor her coffee. She'd been dreamily sipping the rich brew while she divided her attention between the distant hills and the hummingbird that was plundering the red blossoms over her head.

The tiny, dour-faced woman, who was mother of the ranch foreman, consulted a watch she wore pinned to her flat bosom. "The señor will return very soon for lunch," she said, in much the same tone she would have announced the second coming.

Yes, and that was precisely why Kara needed to go. She had avoided Jordan successfully this morning by simply staying in bed late. Knowing his impatience, she had guessed that he would not wait around for her long, and she had been right. He was down at the stables, Mrs. Cavazos had told her with a hint of reproach, when Kara at last came down the stairs.

It had been a restless night for Kara. Though Jordan had been half the house away, she had felt his presence all night long. Had felt his mouth on her lips for hours after that one mocking kiss. Show and tell, she remembered, then pushed angrily away from the table. It was time to grab her suitcase and get out of here. It would be hard enough looking Jordan in the eye the next time she met him. No use making it harder by doing it on his home ground.

But even down the hill Kara felt restless and out of place. After she'd unpacked her suitcase in the groom's apartment, she had nothing to do. Her father and the lumber truck would not arrive for hours yet, even if they'd started at dawn. Well, she wasn't going to sit here waiting. She'd hardly explored the ranch at all. Now was the perfect opportunity.

BUT THE RANCH was too big to explore on foot, Kara concluded some time later—she'd barely scratched its surface. She'd wandered through brood mare barns and foaling barns. Seen a race track with two colts and their riders circling it endlessly. Walked through a stable that housed the young stud that would someday replace Smoky Joe. She'd skirted the yearlings' paddock and watched the long-legged Thoroughbred colts and fillies romping in the distance. She'd stumbled across the main bunkhouse at lunchtime and had been persuaded to sit down on its shady front porch to drink ice tea with Mike Cavazos and some of the hands. When she left, they had pointed the way to the barn where Smoky Joe had been housed since the night of the fire.

The paddock fence was a good eight feel tall. Kara peered through the railings. Joe wasn't in the attached barn, so he must be out here somewhere. The paddock was a big one, and studded with gigantic oaks. Their low-hanging branches cast pools of deep shadow over the thick grass.

She climbed onto the fence for a better look. There! On the far side of the pasture a tail pale as smoke flicked out from behind the trunk of a tree, then vanished. Her lips pursed before she even thought, and she blew that rising, three note whistle she had taught Joe ten long years ago.

A snort sounded in the distance. Would he possibly remember the call? She stepped up to the next railing and whistled once more.

Beyond the oak a head shot up from the grass. She whistled again, and the big head snaked around, as he sought its source with his one good eye.

"Joe!" she called, waving her hand over her head. He snorted, shook his head and sauntered toward her. Laughing aloud, she scrambled over the fence. "Joe!"

As he stepped out of the shade, his size hit her. He had been not quite two the last time she saw him, tall for his age even then, but without the bulk of a mature stallion. The chest that she remembered as being deep but scrawny was now a wall of flowing muscle. The hindquarters that were so high a sportswriter had once compared them to a bobcat's hind end, rippled and thrust him forward in a walk that looked bone-lazy but was carrying him toward her with startling efficiency.

But if he'd filled out, his big gray ears were as mulish as ever. Right now their tips almost touched in an expression of ridiculous, passionate curiosity. *Who and what are you?* those ears were asking.

"Joe, it's me!" she called and walked to meet him.

When she moved, the stud stopped. His big jughead pulled in toward his chest as he arched his neck, and his ears flicked back. She stopped, giving him time to make up his mind. He chopped a forefoot at the ground, sending grass flying, and shook his head nervously. She whistled, softly this time, and his ears pricked. He flowed forward in that odd, ground-eating stride, his head cocked to one side to take her all in.

"Joe, it's me."

He sucked in a massive, snorting breath—a sound of skepticism and downright disapproval.

"Really, it is," she said, not moving as he craned his neck toward her. His velvety muzzle bumped her cheek and she laughed. "See? I told you."

Stepping closer, he blew into her hair, a hot, grassy breath of disgusted agreement. *Yeah, it's you. So where's my carrot?*

"I forgot it, Joe," she crooned, reaching a hand up to rub his white jaw. "Next time, though, I promise."

"Kara!" No one had ever yelled her name on quite that note of outrage. She spun around, and the stud half reared at her movement.

Seated on his blood bay, Jordan Stonehall glared over the fence at her. "Don't *move*!" He swung off the gelding and dropped the reins in a ground hitch. The horse stood waiting, its ears flicking forward toward the stud, then back nervously.

Beside her, Joe lifted his ugly head, his nostrils flaring wide and pink in his dark muzzle. His head wove with an odd snakish movement, and his ears flattened. He glided past Kara toward the fence.

Swearing quietly, Stonehall walked away from his mount down the fenceline. "Okay, start moving and angle in toward me. Slowly."

What was the fuss about? If he wanted a fuss, he should look to his gelding! Smoky Joe neared the fence, his head lowered to his knees and snaking out toward the bay. She looked back to see Stonehall swinging over the rails. His face was pale, jaw muscles bulging. Kara stopped short. That body language was easier to read than any stud's, and if looks could kill . . .

"Get over here!" he snarled, his voice pitched low. He didn't wait for her to *get* but came to fetch her, moving unhurriedly but with a furious intention in every stride that reminded her of the stud. Her heart thumped against her breast, then kept on thumping. She was in trouble this time. She turned as Joe screamed and charged the gelding. "Joe!"

"Kara, so *help* me—be quiet!" He almost jerked her off her feet as he started her toward the fence, guiding her in a direction that carried them away from the two horses.

"He's going to hurt your horse," she gasped, looking over her shoulder.

"He's going to hurt himself. Or us, if we're not lucky." He yanked her savagely to the fence and shoved her at it. "Up."

Down the fenceline, the gelding had decided enough was enough as Joe reared to batter the top rail with his forefeet. Forgetting his training, the bay retreated, his head turned to one side so he wouldn't step on his dragging reins. The stallion screamed his challenge again and wheeled along the fence, turning their way.

"*Move!*" Jordan emphasized the command with a resounding smack to her bottom.

With a yelp of outrage Kara swarmed up the fence and dropped down on the other side. She whirled to face him. "Don't you *ever*—" Her yell turned to a gasp of horror. Jordan had been one step behind her, but his bad arm made him slower. He was still astride the fence, moving fast. The white stud reared above him, his forefeet slashing the air. "*Jordan!*"

She lunged to grab him just as he leaped. They collided in midair, collapsed with grunts of surprise, while the stud's hooves rang on the railing above them. Then Joe was gone, thundering along the fence to follow the fleeing gelding.

Gulping for air, Kara stared into a pair of blazing gray eyes. He didn't seem to have any more wind than she did—he sucked in a breath through clenched teeth. "You idiot!" he panted.

"Me! I was just—" She didn't have enough breath to explain. She pushed on his shoulders, but he didn't roll off her.

"You were just trying to get yourself killed! You don't *ever* approach a strange stud on foot. You're lucky he didn't bite your head off!"

"Joe's not a strange stud. He knows me." She shoved at his shoulders again, but if anything, his solid weight seemed to settle upon her. He was incredibly warm, and his heat was seeping into her. She felt as if she were blushing from the toes up.

Jordan swore softly and shook his head. "I can't believe you! I've had more trouble in the last week than I've had in the last twenty years."

"Well, you're making it for yourself! Joe and I were doing fine till you came along. Now let me *up!*" She smacked his shoulder for emphasis.

"No." Jordan shook his head, but he moved his arms to take a bit of his weight on his elbows. He glared at her.

"*No?*" she repeated. Did he plan to lie here in the dust all day with her?

At the note of outrage in her voice, his lips twitched then straightened again to an implacable line. "Not till you promise me. You don't ever go near Joe again. Not without me around."

"But he was my horse!" And after this, she didn't plan to be around Jordan Stonehall a second more than was necessary.

"Was," Jordan agreed grimly. "He's mine now. So stay away from him. We've had enough accidents around here."

He was so close, she could see his pupils expand. His lashes were as thick as her own, but shorter and darker. As she stared at them, they drooped lower, darkening his eyes. But she couldn't sustain that gaze for long. Her eyes drifted to his lips. Her breathing wasn't working right, though that was hardly surprising, with him lying on top of her. She turned her head, her cheek pressing into the fragrant grass. "Okay, I promise," she muttered. He had to let her up—had to let her up soon. He was so hot. A languid, dreamy heat was coursing through her veins like honey.

But he wasn't done with her yet. He stared at her for one breath, two, then three, each one of them deeper and slower than the one before. "Pouting again?" he asked finally.

"I'm not," she snapped, but still wouldn't look at him.

His chest moved against her with silent laughter, and his hand came up to her face. One finger stroked her bottom lip. "You mean it sticks out that much naturally?"

That brought her head around. He returned her scowl with a faint, teasing grin and touched her lip again. His forefinger smoothed slowly across it, tracing its lush under-curve, then returning along the line between upper and lower.

It came as naturally as breathing to part her lips. His fingertip stroked deeper, found the dampness just within, teased it out to polish the rounded softness. He delved into her dampness again, and this time she bit his fingertip. To punish him, she told herself, knowing as her teeth closed on him delicately and he sucked in a breath, that it was for a different and darker reason altogether.

Jordan glanced up with a start, then rolled off her. "Get up, Kara." He caught her arm and rose, dragging her to her feet. In the distance a rider was approaching. Led by his reins, Jordan's bay loped beside him.

While Jordan strode forward to meet the horseman, Kara stood where she was. She felt dizzy, confused, almost floating with the sudden release from Jordan's pinning weight, dazzled by the sun and the touch of his hands. The cowboy was glancing over Jordan's head at her, and she swung away to hang on tightly to the fence. What had she been thinking, to let him touch her like that? This was a man who would have sent her father to jail without thinking twice, if she hadn't intervened. This was a man who thought she was a child, didn't take her seriously at all.

Which meant that whatever his intentions a minute ago, they'd not been serious. He'd been playing with her. More show and tell. Shaking her head in confusion, she stared through the railings. Smoky Joe had returned to his shade on the far side of the pasture. He glowered at the two riding horses from there, but apparently he'd asserted his supremacy enough for one day. It was awfully hot for temper tantrums.

"Have you seen him move yet?" Jordan asked from beside her.

"Walk, you mean?" She shook her head without turning.

"We'll have to bring him in. Check his legs," Jordan murmured, more to himself than her. He let out an exasperated breath. "Kara, a breeding stud's a moody animal. Joe especially. I don't ride him anymore, so he's pretty full of himself. Far as he knows, he can do whatever he damn well pleases, especially when he's out of his stall."

"He wouldn't have hurt me," she said, her eyes still on the stud.

"Don't give him the chance again." When she didn't speak, he hooked a finger under her chin and brought her face around. Gray eyes probed deep into turquoise. "I have your promise?"

"Yes," she said. She would have said anything to end this encounter.

"Good." His eyes flicked to her lips, then up again. "Want a ride back to your place?"

Behind him on the bay? "No, I . . . I think I'll keep walking."

His mouth curved for a second, as if he knew why she refused. "Fine. See you later, then." He turned and strode off to the gelding, who waited for him a prudent distance from the fence.

Kara stared after his long, lean-hipped form. It wasn't fair. Wasn't fair at all that he could raise such a storm of emotions inside her, and yet be so unaffected himself. If she hadn't had enough reasons to dislike him already, she could have hated him for that alone.

KARA HEARD the truck coming up the hill from the highway long before it reached the crest. With a sigh of relief she left her seat on the parapet on the little humpbacked bridge and walked toward the sound. It was almost sundown. She'd begun to wonder what Jordan would do if Hank didn't arrive today. Would he have insisted she sleep again in the big house?

The large rig topped the hill. She raised her hand and stepped to the side of the road. It groaned to a halt beside her.

"Kara!" Hank leaned out the passenger window. "Are you all right?" He opened his door.

"Of course I am, Dad." She climbed up beside him and gave the driver of the truck a smile. "I'm sorry to run out on you like that." Their shoulders bumped as the truck started off. "You got Jordan's note?"

"Jordan?" His spiky eyebrows climbed up his endless forehead.

"Mr. Stonehall," she corrected herself. "You got it?"

"Oh, I got it all right," Hank growled. "About eight last night, when the blasted desk clerk came back from supper. Till then I was some worried." He patted her knee. "You sure you're all right, girl?"

"Yes, of course I am." The truck was passing the house now. Kara looked up at the shadowed gallery on the second floor and saw a figure stir against the lights beyond. She lifted her chin defiantly, though it wasn't likely Jordan could see her. So now you know, she told him silently. We keep our word.

"That blasted Stonehall," her father growled. "He really thought we were running out on him? That's why he took you back?"

"Reckon so." Even though she'd felt exactly the same way herself, his anger was making her uncomfortable. But then, when had she last been comfortable? It wasn't only a barn they'd burned down the other night. She felt as if her peace of mind had gone up in smoke as well.

"Well, that does it! I've got a good mind to just dump this load and go. If a man won't take you at your word—"

"Dad, even if we hadn't made a promise, we've got no place to go."

"I don't know about that. I've been thinking, Kara. If there's one thing I know, it's wood. Maybe we ought to take a look at East Texas. What do you think, Harry?" He turned to the driver. "Think there's enough room for another sawmill, 'round your neck of the woods?"

Harry just grinned politely and shrugged, but Kara shook her head impatiently. "Dad, that's just talk and you know it." She couldn't point out to him in front of the driver that they had no money to start a sawmill, or that Smitty's mill had looked pretty down and out to her. With Texas in the middle of an oil bust, building was hardly a booming industry.

"Well, it was just a thought . . ." he mumbled, sounding a little hurt.

She nodded and patted his gnarled hand. It was only a dream. And what was wrong with that? Maybe that's all some folks have, she told the image of Jordan Stonehall that floated into her mind. He was smiling his half-contemptuous smile. Oh, she knew what he'd say all right. That Hank ought to dream a little less and do a little more.

A man makes his own luck, a male voice murmured dryly in her head. She gritted her teeth, and shook her head to make him go away.

"KARA, I WAS crazy," Hank said panting. "I should never have got you into this." He sank to the foundation beside his daughter. "Last time I built this thing, I had manpower. We'd have just picked up that darned timber and moved it."

Too winded herself to speak, Kara nodded and stared at the beam. They had made a mistake, unloading in the twilight last night. Hank had had it all planned out, where each of the massive timbers would be placed around the foundation. The idea was to minimize the need to move any of the heavy stock. So with the help of the timber truck's crane, they had laid out the wood according to plan. But this morning, by the light of day, their mistake was painfully obvious. They had placed the wrong timber up on the foundation.

So they'd spent the last hour moving it out of the way, then fighting the fourteen by fourteen they needed into place. Lacking the six hefty workmen her father remembered so fondly, they'd done it the hard way, using jacks to lift it over anything in its path. Now they were using two block and tackle come-alongs to drag it to the foundation.

This will take forever, Kara thought despairingly. "It's almost there," she said, comforting him. But if they were having so much trouble with one timber, how were they going to raise whole sections of the barn at one time? *We'll never do it*.

But they had to. While they jacked the beam up, she talked to cheer him, telling him in short snatches about the flight back from Beaumont. "It was *beautiful*. Houston looked like the Milky Way, like you were looking down at the stars instead of up... Imagine just being able to get in a plane and go! You could fly to Austin for lunch... Or run over to Dallas to see how Eddy and Bill like their new job."

The timber was at the proper height, with blocks of wood stacked underneath to keep it there.

Hank looked at her and shook his head mournfully.

"Why are you looking so down at the mouth?" she asked.

"I was just wishing I could give you a plane, if that's what you want. This isn't the kind of life I wanted for you, Kara—working harder than a roustabout. I wanted you to have the best things in life—airplanes, fancy restaurants, shopping at Nieman Marcus. And here I haven't even sent you to college. If I hadn't been such a damn *fool*, letting go of Smoky Joe..."

"Dad..." She came to sit on the timber beside him. "What are you talking about? You *gave* me the best things in life. You've given me somebody who cares about me through thick and thin. You've taught me to work hard and to be proud of my work. You've showed me how to keep my chin up, come what may. What's an old airplane to all that?"

"I promised your mother I'd send you to college," he muttered.

"I tried college, remember? I could have stayed on, if I'd wanted to." She had wanted to. But he had needed her, and if she was all he had, then it cut the other way as well. Family was more important than college. She'd get the education some day. Somehow. "Now stop worrying and come on. This barn isn't going to build itself." She knelt beside the timber, getting her shoulder under its edge. They counted it together. "One, two... *heave!*" Kara pushed till she thought her shoulder would crack, and then the log turned. "One more," she gasped.

"Hey! Hang on there, let me give you a hand!" a tenor voice sang out. Kara turned to see Chris Haley striding toward them with a mare and chestnut foal trotting at his heels. He stopped to tie them to a stack of barn board by the long halter rope that connected the pair together, then hurried over. "You all shouldn't move that thing by yourselves! Somebody's bound to rupture something for sure."

With Chris's broad shoulder added to the load, the timber rolled smoothly into place.

"Thanks, Chris," Kara said when she stood to introduce her father. As the men shook hands, the cowboy's gaze panned around the foundation. His cheerful eyes widened as they took in the massive posts and beams.

"Where's your crew?" he asked bluntly.

"You're looking at it," Kara said before Hank could speak, then changed the subject. "Can I pet your baby there?" She started toward the foal.

"Why sure." He followed her as she'd hoped. The little one had seized the break in its training for a snack. It was butting the mare's udder enthusiastically, its whisk broom tail switching with gusto. She ran a hand down its baby-soft back, earning a long measuring look from its mother, but the filly ignored her completely.

"She's one of Joe's?" she asked, as Chris untied the mare.

"Look at that rear end and the length of those legs," he agreed with a grin. As he started the mare moving, the baby popped up from under its dam with a look of comical surprise. He caught the rope near its tiny halter. "Want to walk with me a ways? I've got half a dozen of these tykes to walk before lunch time."

"Dad?" she called, turning to her father.

He waved her off. "Take a break, Kara."

"Can I lead the little one?" she asked Chris.

He handed her one end of the halter rope. "Long as you don't let her know she's being led. She just thinks she's out for a stroll with mama."

Kara laughed. "She's awfully young for halter breaking, isn't she?"

"Not by Stonehall's book," he drawled. "But don't let him hear you call it that. There ain't no breaking about it, his way. It's all gentle persuasion. They're doing what he wants before they even notice."

Remembering the way he'd manipulated her to fly with him, she grimaced. She could well believe it. She ran a hand up the filly's mane. "I think she's going to be prettier than her daddy," she said lightly.

"I surely hope so," Chris agreed with a twinkle. "The boss man is always working on that, every pairing he makes. That's the problem in a nutshell—how to breed in some looks, without losing the heart and the speed. 'Round here we say ol' Joe runs like the devil, but he looks like him, too." They walked a little farther down the road, then Kara turned.

"Guess I'd better get back to work." She handed him the lead line. "Thanks, Chris."

"Anytime." He smiled at her, then cast a worried look toward the barn. "Kara...it ain't any of my business, but what the heck are you all trying to prove?" he blurted. "That's a man-size job back there."

She didn't want to talk about it, and her face must have told him so. "We said we'd do it, and we will, Chris," she said with a shrug. Somehow.

"I'd sure come help you, but Mike Cavazos rides us pretty close..."

"Thanks just the same, Chris." She gave the foal's rump a final pat.

"Now wait a minute!" Chris called, as she turned away. "Maybe I can help!" His face had lit with pleasure. "Would a power winch do you all any good? I drive an old Jeep. It's got a winch on the front bumper you could pull an elephant out of a mudhole with."

"Could we!" With a winch like that they could drag timbers wherever they needed them. "But..." She bit her lip. "Dad's not much for borrowing. He says a good carpenter has his own tools and doesn't mooch."

Chris laughed as he dragged a key ring out of his pocket. "Kara, you tell him about that million-dollar baby my mare is going to drop. Far as I'm concerned, I figure I owe you." He caught the hand that hung by her side, and put the key ring in it. "It's parked down by the bunkhouse," he said. "You use it every day, if you need to. It's just sitting there."

Her fingers closed around the keys, hard and tight. They could do it. With Chris's winch, they just might be able to do it! "Chris, I don't know how to—" But if she couldn't think what to say, her gratitude still needed an outlet. Standing on tiptoe, she gave him a smacking kiss on the cheek. "You don't know what this means!" She patted his raw-boned shoulders ecstatically and spun away. If this didn't put the heart back in her father—

Kara stopped short. Near the foundation, a horseman sat a rangy gray colt. Her father stood beside the Thoroughbred, glaring at its rider. But Jordan Stonehall paid him no heed. Even at this distance there was a lift to his chin that told her he'd witnessed her exuberant kiss. But why he should look so grim about it, she could not imagine.

CHAPTER SEVEN

HE WAS FURIOUS with her. Again. Though his face was almost expressionless, she could feel his anger warming her skin as if she walked toward the flames of a bonfire.

She didn't flatter herself that he could be jealous—he'd made it all too plain that he thought she was only a kid. *So why should you care if I flirt with another nice kid like Chris Haley?* she thought rebelliously as she stopped shoulder to shoulder with Hank and looked up to meet Jordan's narrowed eyes.

Or maybe that wasn't what was bothering him at all. Maybe he thought she'd been keeping Chris from his work, or— Maybe she would just ask. "What seems to be the problem, Mr. Stonehall?" she asked, some inner devil making her goad him with the formal salute.

But he was in no mood for teasing. His lips tightened, and the young gray tossed its head uneasily as it caught its rider's mood. "I was asking your dad where his construction crew was," he replied.

Oh, lord, so that was it! She should have anticipated this. Instead she'd looked on the lack of a crew as her and Hank's problem to be overcome, without considering that Jordan would disapprove. "You're looking at his crew!" she said with an impudent grin to cover her worry.

"All hundred and five pounds of it," Jordan growled, his eyes sweeping her from her painter's cap to her small white sneakers. He shook his head, turned to scan the tons of wood lying like a felled forest around them and shook his head again. "Against all this? No way, half-pint. That's not what I thought I was getting, at all."

"I told you you were getting a barn, is what I told you!" Hank spoke so suddenly, that both of his listeners jumped, as if they'd forgotten he was part of this confrontation. "How we deliver that barn is our business."

"If anyone's hurt on this ranch, it's my business," Jordan disagreed. "And this is no job for two people." His eyes flicked to Kara. "For one and a half."

At the insult her hands clenched into fists and she stepped to the gray's shoulder, some vague desire to pummel Jordan's kneecap driving her forward. But the gesture spooked the colt. It skittered sideways, nearly trampling Hank in the process.

With a wordless snarl, Jordan steadied him with rein and thigh. Kara stole a glance at her father. He looked ready to explode on her behalf. And Jordan's temper clearly burned on a short fuse. Let these two really start butting heads, and there'd be no stopping them.

"Dad…" Turning to her father, she dropped the keys she was holding into his hand. "Chris wants to loan us his Jeep, to help us build the barn. It has a winch on the front end. He wants you to follow him right now, so he can show you how to use it." *Leave this to me,* she pleaded silently. She could handle Jordan, if anyone could.

"I don't like borrowing," Hank grumbled. But her request had distracted him, and a light was beginning to gleam in his hazel eyes. A winch—yes, he was seeing the possibilities already. His eyes switched back to Stonehall. "But we still have to settle—"

"I can settle it," she cut in urgently. She sighed in relief as he nodded—one short, reluctant jerk of his head that included both her and the rider glaring down at them, then swung away.

They watched him stump off up the rise, and Kara felt an odd sense of union for a moment, as if Jordan shared her relief in Hank's going. When her dad was out of earshot, they turned as one to glare at each other.

"No," Jordan growled. "No way, Kara."

"I'm getting a crick in my neck looking at you," she countered. If she was going to fight him, she would need every bit of advantage she could glean. No use letting him play King of the Mountain.

But when he swung down off the colt, he did so in one lithe move that turned all the arguments she'd been marshaling to a jumble of words in her head. She had to turn her back on him while he tied the gray off. Struggling to drive that unexpected hunger from her mind, she tried to remember that here was the enemy, and that for Hank's sake, she had to bend him to her will. She found herself staring at one of the massive cross beams, and then, with a wry smile, she stepped up onto it. She turned to find herself nose to nose with Jordan.

One corner of his mouth twitched, then went straight again. "No," he said. "Not even if you grew a foot. No, and no, and no again."

Something about the word was hypnotizing her. Or maybe it was just the movement of his lips as he shaped the word. She forced her eyes away to meet his. "You owe me."

"No."

"Yes, you do." She wouldn't forget in a year, or a hundred years, the feel of his chest, hard and slippery with sweat and blood. Her triumph when he was safe at last. Holding him in her arms while the fire burned.

"That's not what I mean and you know it." Scowling, he yanked his hat off and smacked it against his thigh. "I mean no, you can't build the barn. I'll pay you back some other way, Kara. But not this way."

"This is the only way I want, Jordan Stonehall." She wanted to take hold of his shoulders—to shake him, to yank him to her so that he'd read it in her eyes. "This is the only payment I'll take. You owe me. You owe *us* the chance to pay you back. We can do it."

"You're going to raise a barn? You can't even lift that beam you're standing on!"

"Oh, yeah?" This time she couldn't resist the urge to touch him. She pointed her finger at him, then jabbed it lightly into his chest. "I'll show you!" She jumped off the beam and scanned the ground for what she needed.

He caught her arm and spun her around. "Kara, dammit, that's the last thing I want—you wrecking your back trying to prove something. That's why I'm stopping this farce."

She wrenched away from him. "I'll raise that beam the same way Dad and I are going to raise your barn, *Mr.* Stonehall!" The jack was lying on the ground not far away. She scooped up its compact weight and returned to the timber, blessing Hank's forethought in blocking one end of each beam off the ground. The jack fit under it nicely. Grasping the jack handle, she looked up at him. "How high would you like it?" she asked sweetly.

With a growl of exasperation, he caught her arms and lifted her. "Okay, so you're a clever girl. You can lift a beam with a jack. But we're not talking games or parlor tricks when it comes to a barn. We're talking about tons of wood rising up into the air at one time. We're talking one slip and somebody's smashed flat, Kara. You can have all the mechanical advantage in the world, but if a winch fails, or a rope breaks, or—"

"You owe me." It was odd to be held in such a firm grasp and yet to feel that she was holding him. But she was—with her words, her eyes, her unswerving determination. For this moment as she tipped her head to meet his furious gaze, they were locked together body and soul.

"You are the most mule-headed . . . brat!" He shook her once, but gently, as if he didn't dare vent the frustration trembling within his hands.

"Woman," she corrected softly. "I'm the most mule-headed *woman*."

He pushed her back a step and let her go. "You're just like your father, that's what you are!"

"What do you mean by that?" For a moment as he held her, she'd felt complete, at one with her world, powerful enough to match him. As he pushed her away, the feeling passed. She felt small and uncertain. Young.

"You're a dreamer. Impractical. A drifter like he is. Dreams are fine for night, Kara, but you shouldn't try to bring them into the real world. This barn—this is reality, sweetheart. And reality can come down pretty hard and fast."

"I am not a dreamer. And neither is Dad!"

"You are, short stuff, if you think you can build this barn, just the two of you. You're making promises you can't keep."

"We'll keep them."

But he wasn't listening. "Life isn't about making promises, Kara. Life is about *delivering* on them. Me, I've heard enough promises to last me a life-time." For a second, his eyes looked right through her, to someone else, somewhere else, some broken promise.

"Maybe other people work that way, but not me. I deliver when I make a promise. So does my dad."

"Oh, yeah?" he jeered. "I bet he promised that you'd race Smoky Joe in the Kentucky Derby, when you owned him. Did he ever deliver on that one? And what about that division of houses that went bankrupt in Kerrville?"

He had it all wrong. She shook her head, but he forged on.

"The man has no follow-through, that's his problem, and when things go wrong, he doesn't look for solutions, he looks for excuses. 'It was the Stonehalls' fault. The barn was unlucky.'"

"For him maybe it was!"

"Makes me wonder if that's not what's happening here— if I'm being set up. When he finds he can't build this barn, he'll end up blaming me again, won't he?"

"But that won't happen. We're going to build this barn."

"No." It was his final word, the way he said it. She felt as if he'd punched her over the heart with it, and something in her eyes must have mirrored the blow. At least his face softened as he looked down at her. He touched a lock of hair that had escaped her barrette to curl across her cheek. "No," he repeated, his voice husky with regret. He turned on his heel and started for the colt.

No. No, she wouldn't let it end this way. Not after they'd come so far. Taking a deep breath, she ran after him, caught at his arm. "No!" she said breathlessly. "No, you can't *do* this. What about your promise to Dad?"

Slowly he swung around. "My promise, Kara?"

"You told him he could rebuild your barn! What good is *your* word, Jordan Stonehall, if you go back on that?"

"He didn't make things clear, Kara. If he'd told me he had no crew—"

"Did you ask?" She pushed his arm. "Did you?"

Grimly he shook his head. "No, I didn't think—"

"And did you bother to think where we got the money for this wood? We sold our truck to buy this wood. Because we were depending on your word that we'd need it to build the barn. What good is all this wood to us, if you've changed your mind? We can't drive it away from here."

"You sold your *truck*?"

But that wasn't what was important. Her fingers dug into resilient muscle as she shook his arm. "Don't you see? That wasn't just your barn that we burned. It was my *dad's* barn. I don't give a damn about you, Jordan Stonehall—he needs to rebuild it for him! You've got to let us do it. You gave your word we could."

"I see," he said tightly. They both glanced up as a battered Jeep came bumping over the rise from the direction of the bunkhouse. "I see..." Jordan murmured again, more to himself than her. He took a deep breath. "You have to assemble all the parts of the barn before you put it up, don't you?"

"Yes." Hank had spelled it out for her, step by step.

"When's the earliest you'll be ready to raise her?"

"Dad figured late next week sometime."

The rancher settled his hat on his head and nodded grimly. "All right...we'll take it a step at a time. You can keep working till I come back—on one condition."

"Back?" He was going away? She could feel the shock of that hitting her face, and she dropped her eyes. Looking down, she found she was holding his arm in what must have been a painful grip. She let go, but her fingers were stiff from being curled so tight. Her hand stroked the length of his arm in a clumsy, sliding caress as it dropped away. Her face flushed, and his eyes seemed to darken as he swayed nearer.

"Yes, I'm off to the yearling sales in Kentucky. I'll be back in ten days."

Ten days. That seemed a very long time.

"So I want your promise, Kara, if you're so good at keeping promises." He tipped a knuckle under her chin to bring her face up, as if he could read the answer in her eyes. "You don't raise that barn without me, is that understood?"

"Yes," she whispered. The Jeep's door slammed nearby, but she couldn't look away from his eyes. Black and silver, they seemed to be sliding into her, gently and irrevocably, as a dagger glides into a heart. Oh, she didn't want him to go, not now. Not ever.

"And you understand that I can stop this nonsense anytime I want?"

It was so unfair. He could stop the way he felt. Turn it off or on as it pleased him. While she... something was finding its final shape inside of her, something that would stand there like a barn, solid and true and forever, if some fool didn't burn it to the ground.

"And that I will stop it, if it endangers anyone? You understand?"

Kara nodded again. She understood—that she was endangered past saving.

His knuckle slid away, stroking the side of her jaw as it went. Jordan stood there for a second, simply looking at her. Then, as if something in her face had satisfied him, he nodded. "Then take care till I return," he almost whispered. He touched a finger to his hat brim and turned away. He nodded stiffly at Hank as he passed him, but he didn't stop to talk. Collecting the colt, he swung into the saddle with that same heart-stopping grace, and rode off. And he didn't look back even once.

WITH SO MUCH to do, the time should have gone quickly. Instead, once Jordan had gone, the ten days seemed to stretch out into an endless span of waiting. But Kara had plenty to do.

The four massive foundation timbers, the "sills" on which the whole barn would rest, had to be joined together at the corners of the structure. It was a pleasure to watch Hank cut the two halves of a dovetail joint into two sills, then see them interlock with a gapless precision that seemed to astound and delight him almost as much as it did her. At least, at first it seemed to astound him. By the second day, Hank's hesitations and nervousness seemed to have vanished. He worked with a sort of dreaming, unquestioning intensity, as if he were listening to a voice inside his head. His expression reminded Kara of what he'd said once. *It was like that barn wanted to be built, Kara. Like the timbers almost stood up and marched into place. It was magic.* Well, magic or not, it *felt* like magic to see him working better and faster and surer with each task that he completed. By the end of the second day, the sills were laid and joined.

Next came the big fifty-foot girder that had to be laid lengthwise down the center of the floor frame. Without Chris's Jeep, it would have been impossible to move it into place. Even with the Jeep's winch, the job was horrendous. They had too many beams laid out around the foundation to be able to drive the Jeep where they needed it. But then Mike Cavazos rode by at midday and noticed their problem. That evening, the foreman returned in the ranch truck with two other hands and four steel drums.

Once Mike had welded tops on each of the drums, they made excellent rollers. "It's almost better than six men," Hank decided the first time they tried it. Mike and his men provided a grinning audience.

With Jordan out of the way, the Tates were seeing more of his employees. Kara couldn't decide if the men's increasing sociability meant that Jordan had ordered them not to

befriend the Tates, and now that he was gone, they were ig-
noring those orders. Or maybe it was simply that it had
taken them a while to decide where she and her father fit
into the scheme of things, and now they had passed some
unspoken test. Or maybe it was simply the day by day evo-
lution of the barn that attracted the men.

Whatever the reason, someone was always stopping by at
lunchtime to see if the Tates could use some extra muscle.
Once they moved into the stage of cutting the mortises—the
notches in the sills into which the floor joists would fit—
Chris or Mike or any one of half a dozen others would show
up in the evening to watch Hank do the rough cuts with the
big saber saw. They found it even more fun to watch Kara
finish the cuts with her mortise and corner chisels.

"I swear I think we should charge 'em for watching,"
Hank grumbled as he and Kara paused to take a breather
and look around. "If I had a nickel for every time I've explained what I'm doing..." Across the foundation, Mike
Cavazos and two other men sat on the sill, smoking and
talking idly. Bare-chested and sweating even though the sun
had just set, Chris Haley and a hand called Lew were trun-
dling one of the floor joists to where Hank and Kara would
fasten it in place.

"They're having fun," Kara told him. And she would
have been having fun too, if there hadn't been a persistent
gnawing inside her. She'd been going over and over her last
fight with Jordan. There were so many things she wished
she'd said. He thought she was a drifter, did he? Somehow
she had to make him see that wasn't so. That this gypsy ex-
istence of following Hank from job to job around the hill
country had been a matter of economic survival, not her
choice of the way to live—couldn't he see that?

And he thought she was like Hank, someone with no follow-through, a dreamer. Well, maybe Hank had dreamed

his share of impractical dreams, but that had only made her the more practical from an early age.

Until now. Now, as Kara worked, she found herself dreaming constantly. What if somehow, someway, she made Jordan see that she wasn't a child?

But then who was she kidding? A man with his sophistication and wealth falling for a little undereducated nobody like her? Why, right this minute at the yearling sales he'd be rubbing elbows with the kinds of women that were a proper match for him. Blue-blood Kentucky debs, or heiresses from New York come to fling a few million on a race colt.

"Well, they ain't seen nothing yet," Hank growled, breaking into her misery. "The fun has only just begun. Tomorrow we start building the bents."

The bents—they were what a person pictured when he heard the words *barn-raising*—the big open frameworks rising up into the air, men pushing and pulling to lift them upright. There would be five bents in the Stonehall barn, spaced about twelve and a half feet apart.

"Back in the old days, a barn was the most valuable thing most families owned," Hank told her when they'd completed the first one. "They made 'em so they could be taken down and moved, if the family moved on. Ol' man Stonehall showed me a book once that talked about that."

Kara was careful not to turn to him too quickly. "He was interested in architecture?" She had often wondered what Jordan's father had been like.

"Had a bee in his bonnet about it," Hank grunted. "Seems there'd been an even older barn on this spot, back when the Germans built the big house. He wanted something that would look and feel as if it had been built 'bout the same time. Wouldn't hear of us using a nail in the whole darn building."

Kara smiled to herself. Hank had been defending himself yesterday against Chris's skepticism on the same subject. It seemed that old man Stonehall's lust for authenticity was a contagious disease.

By the end of the week even Chris seemed to have caught the architectural bug. He stopped for his daily inspection late in the day, while Kara and Hank were completing the fifth and final bent. "Fits together sweet as you please," he drawled as they hammered the last post onto the waiting tenons of the cross beams. The mare he was holding stretched her nose toward the frames and inhaled deeply, then snorted at the smell of fresh wood chips. Her black filly did a tiny buck and shy, as Hank stood and stretched his back. Chris gave her a little more rope.

"You wouldn't have said so if you'd seen us at lunchtime," Kara laughed. "I didn't cut a mortise quite wide enough, and the post stuck, half on it, half off. Surprised you didn't hear us snarling, all the way to the bunkhouse." She nodded quick agreement as Hank murmured something about grabbing a snack for them both and headed toward the foaling barn.

"I meant to stop by to see how y'all were coming 'bout then, but the boss man's been working us so hard all morning, I reckoned I'd better sit and blow awhile, when I got the chance."

"Stonehall's back?" Her spirits rocketed skyward, then, like a rocket, found their high point and tumbled end over end back to earth. He'd been here all morning and hadn't bothered to come see her?

"Yeah, he flew in about ten," Chris agreed. "And he landed running. Guess the leisure life don't agree with some folks."

He hadn't taken the time to stop by. She dropped the mallet she'd been holding and wiped a forearm across her hot forehead. But then, why should he want to see her? To him, she was nothing but a kid. A very hot and grubby carpenter's kid, today. Well who cares about him, either? she thought fiercely. She looked around to find Chris talking again.

"...could buy an acre along a creek somewhere for not too much. Reckon I could build the house myself, after watching you two..."

A drink of cool water, that's what she needed to wash this taste of bitterness from her mouth. Kara stood, nodding at what Chris was saying, only half hearing it. "Sure you could, Chris." As she stood, she could see over the mare's back.

A bay gelding loped their way, a smaller white filly cantering side by side with him. The filly had no rider, but on the back of the bay... There was no mistaking that easy seat in the saddle. Jordan.

Suddenly she didn't want to see him. Not now, not as dusty and sad as she was feeling all at once. She spun away and stumbled over the cross beam on the ground at her feet. *"Ooops!"*

For all his easy-going ways, Chris could move fast when he wanted. As she fell, he hooked one long arm around her waist. Her momentum carried her almost to the ground, then he dipped her like a tango dancer, her body arching supplely backward, as her hat flew off. "Gotcha!"

Laughing breathlessly as he swooped her back up to the vertical, she grabbed at his shoulders. *"Hoooo!* What a save." Her hairclip had come loose. She shook the hair out of her eyes. "Where did you learn to dance like that?" And then she remembered Jordan. Lips still parted in laughter she turned in Chris's arms to look over her shoulder.

Jordan sat his bay like a statue, his eyes ablaze with cold fire.

Abruptly Chris let her go—he had seen Jordan, too—and Kara staggered as she caught her balance.

"You're tending the wrong filly," Jordan rasped. His chin jerked beyond them.

Kara turned around and gasped. Left to her own devices while Chris was saving her, the black mare had led her foal in among the bents. The mare herself was probably in no danger, but if she should panic and decide to run... The filly was tethered to her. If she should be yanked off balance by her mother and stumble on the timbers, her slender legs could snap like toothpicks.

"*Easy* girl..." Chris was moving already, talking in a low, honeyed drawl. "Easy, you grass guzzler, where do you think you're taking that baby, you jughead? Yeah, I'm talking to *you*. Easy..." The mare leaned away from him, bracing her front feet, clearly contemplating a sudden dodge. "Don't you *dare*, you ol' she-devil..." Hand outstretched he put heart and soul into that warning. At the same moment the foal decided it was feeding time and nudged at her udder. Perhaps that, rather than Chris's pleas, made her hold her ground. He caught the halter rope.

Kara let out her breath and turned to Jordan. "Jordan, that was *my*—"

"Stay out of this." His words cut like a bullwhip. He didn't spare her a glance, his eyes were drilling holes in the ranch hand.

A red-faced Chris led the mare and foal slowly toward them.

"Haley."

Chris swallowed and met his eyes. "Sir?"

"I see you wooing on the job again, you're gone," Jordan said quietly. "Keep your mind on business."

Chris's face went from pink to scarlet, and his head came up dangerously. But his boss had already turned away.

"No!" Kara whispered fiercely. She could see Chris was about to answer back, and it would be his job for sure, with Jordan in this black mood. Then there was no more need for whispering. Jordan's bay and the white filly he led thundered up the road toward the big house.

Chris swore bitterly. "Damn it all to hell, he can't talk to me that way! And damned if I don't tell him so!"

"No, Chris, you can't! You know how much you like this job." She patted his shoulder desperately. "It was my fault. I'll tell him so."

"It wasn't your fault neither! It was nobody's fault. Well, maybe I shouldn't have let go the mare, but still— The man will be watching me like a hawk from now on. He's not big on second chances. I've a good mind to quit and save him the trouble."

"Look, Chris, it was my fault. He's mad at me, and you were just handy to yell at. I'm going to talk to him. Right now."

"What's he mad at you for?" Chris asked sullenly.

She had only said that to make him feel better, but now that she examined the statement, Kara knew it was true. If looks could have killed... But as to why? She shrugged. "It's a long story, Chris. Now, any idea where he was heading?" If she was going to have to do some lion taming she might as well get on with it.

CHAPTER EIGHT

CHRIS HAD SAID Jordan would be at the creek. He hadn'
explained that Jordan would be *in* the creek. Kara found
him upstream of the swimming hole. He was riding away
from her, his bay and the filly that pranced beside his horse
knee-deep in the water. The pair moved at a smart trot
stepping high as they fought the current, sheets of spray
splashing out before them. Jordan had snugged the filly in
so close to his gelding that there was no room for his right
leg between them. Instead he rested his boot on the filly'
saddle. The horses rounded a bend in the creek and passed
out of sight behind a thicket of wild plum. Kara hurried her
steps.

But by the time she rounded the bend, he was some
hundred yards ahead. The creek had deepened, and the water almost brushed the bellies of the horses. Even from thi
distance, she could see that Jordan's blue shirt was wet to
the shoulders. She stopped. She would never catch him a
this rate. But as she wondered if she should yell, if he would
even hear her over the horses' splashing, he turned his pai
around and started back.

With a gasp of relief, Kara moved a few feet up the hil
and sat in a patch of grass to watch.

Sitting as still as she was, he didn't see her at first. Tha
suited her fine. She'd never really had the chance to simpl
stare at him before. To admire the width of his shoulders
to savor the way he tapered to that lean waist and hips, th

grace with which he sat his horse. As he neared, she could
see his expression under his hat brim.

Black mood was the word for it. He was someplace far
away right now, his face set hard against some frustration
or pain that she couldn't imagine. Funny, how she'd always
thought that people like him, people with all the wealth in
the world, had no problems. But Jordan Stonehall was
looking inward at some very big problem right now. Was
driving his horses near to exhaustion while he mulled it over.
The filly tried to slow down—the water was deeper on her
than the bay, but Jordan clamped his thighs tight to urge the
bay on, and the filly was dragged along.

The gelding spotted her before Jordan did. But when
those black-tipped ears flicked in her direction, Jordan's
head swung around. The bay checked his stride as if his
rider's hand had tensed on the reins, then leaped forward
again as he was squeezed back into motion. Jordan gave her
a tight, grim nod, and the horses splashed by.

But they would be returning, Kara realized. Whatever
Jordan's purpose in half drowning his horses, he wasn't
going to take the filly into the deep swimming hole beyond.

When they returned, she was waiting on the bank. "What
are you doing?" she asked as they came abreast of her.

She thought for a moment that he wouldn't stop, and then
he reined in. The white filly heaved a deep sigh of relief, then
stood there blowing hard. Jordan reached down to smooth
a hand along the fine arch of her neck. "I'm getting ready
to saddle break her," he said shortly. As he spoke, he leaned
more of his weight onto the leg that rested across the filly's
saddle. Her delicate ears swung back in startlement, but she
was too tired to object.

"I wanted to talk to you," Kara said when he didn't go
on.

"There's no need, Kara." He clucked and the bay stepped out.

She moved along the bank beside them and raised her voice over the splashing. "Yes, there is a need. That wasn't Chris's fault back there. I tripped and he caught me. That's all it was."

"He should have let you fall on your sweet fanny before he let go of that mare, Kara. And that's between me and him. Stay out of it." He clucked again and the horses moved faster. Kara broke into a jog.

"No, I won't stay out of it! You think he was wooing me—you said so yourself. And I just want you to know that that wasn't what was happening there."

"Sweetheart, when are you going to grow up?" Jordan had raised his voice as well. "A man doesn't have to bring you candy and flowers to be courting you. It's written all over Haley. He looks like a lovesick calf. And that's fine. If I was his age I'd probably chase you myself."

"But—"

"But I'm damned if he's going to neglect his job because he's in love. If that filly had broken a leg..." Scowling, he shook his head, clucked again, and the bay picked up the pace.

Kara stopped. She was not going to make a fool of herself by running along the bank, trying to shout. She'd made far too much of a fool of herself already. She blinked her eyes rapidly, fighting a sudden, treacherous burning behind her lids. So he didn't give a damn about her. It hadn't been jealousy—he didn't care in the least if Chris was courting her—which he wasn't, but that wasn't the point. Jordan didn't care. All he cared about was the blasted foal. She rubbed a forearm viciously across her eyes. How could she have been such a fool? To have hoped, for even one second?

Well, get it out of your head! she told herself bitterly. Little idiot. A hot and grubby little idiot. She'd moved too fast for the heat of the day, traveling here, and the last few minutes had been the final straw. She was almost as soaked as the poor filly. She turned to see that Jordan was still riding away from her, just rounding the bend now.

Well, if he didn't care for her, she was just going to have to cultivate the same attitude. Somehow. She wasn't going to care for him. She wasn't going to care what he thought. What he wanted. *Certainly* wasn't going to waste time feeling sorry for the man when he had a bad mood. *It's me first from now on, Jordan,* she thought grimly.

And if it was her first, then the first thing she could do for herself was have a bath. Her eyes swept over the creek. Or a nice cool swim. And tough cookie if Jordan didn't approve! Yanking off her tennis shoes, she dropped them on the bank and stepped into the river, clothes and all.

By the time the horses rounded the bend and started back again, Kara's temper had improved considerably. There was nothing more soothing than cool, clean water. It was deeper along the far bank, and she was breast stroking along, stopping occasionally to dip like a dolphin all the way under, her hair loose and streaming behind her. The pain in her heart had faded to a dull roar. It was still there, but she didn't have to face it right now. Right now she would simply concentrate on the glitter of late sunlight on water, the blue dragonfly that hovered as if he might land in her hair, the sliding, gliding freedom of the river rippling past her cheek.

As Jordan neared her, she stood, waist deep in the water, motionless so she'd not spook his horses. His chin came up as he saw her, and the horses pricked their ears, but they were too tired to take exception to the strange sight of a woman standing mid-creek.

Kara glanced down at her body. She was wearing a dark T-shirt, thank heavens, so it hadn't gone transparent on her. But the water's coolness had brought her small breasts to full and taut arousal. Automatically her arms started to rise, as the instinct to cover herself awoke. But she fought the impulse and simply stood, head lifted proudly and arms at her sides. If he thought she was just a kid, what did he care? He might not have the sense to see her as a woman in a woman's body, but she was damned if she was going to help him continue that crazy notion.

"What the blazes are you doing?" he growled as he came within voice range. He reined in the horses.

"What does it look like? This feels delicious." Slowly she waded toward him. The white filly was on the side facing her. "She's a love," she crooned as she drew near, her voice pitched for the filly's ears. "She's Joe's?"

"Who else?" he muttered sullenly.

"She's so beautiful though. Poor darling, she's all tuckered out." Kara put out her hand. The filly lipped her, then rested her delicate muzzle against her palm as if too tired to hold her head up. "When are you going to break her?"

"Tomorrow. Mike gave Lew the day off, and he's going to be the lucky boy. She's too small for anyone else. It's too bad, she's ready right now."

The desire came from nowhere, full blown. She felt her eyes rounding with it. "I don't weigh much," she said, looking up at him.

He laughed, but there was an undercurrent of anger to it. "No, Kara. Can you even ride?"

"Of course I can ride! The first horse I ever rode was Joe. Imagine starting on the finest horse in the whole world?" she crooned to the filly. The filly bumped her gently, and she laughed and rubbed the hot neck.

"You rode Joe? No wonder it was so easy to break him. I thought that was because of his blindness."

"I used to sit on his back in the stall for hours at a time." She looked up at him again. "Please, Jordan? She's such a beauty. Couldn't I ride her? Grant me this one wish?"

His breath hissed out between his teeth, and his eyes traveled down over her body as if he couldn't stop himself. He shook his head, but the gesture seemed to be aimed inward. "All right," he said grimly. "Come around to the other side."

She could feel her mouth curving into a blissful grin as she waded around the horses. She would have danced with delight and excitement if she'd stood on dry land. "Okay, what now?" she asked as she stopped on the bay's left side.

"Come up." He twisted in the saddle to extend his good hand. "In front of me—not behind."

Delight faded into something else. Somehow she hadn't foreseen— He jerked his hand once impatiently, and she put her own into it, felt his warm fingers envelop her own.

Though he leaned far back in the saddle, it was an awkward way of mounting. She had to bend her right leg to pass it between them, and even so, her calf rubbed across his chest from knee to ankle as she did so. His breath hissed again, as if that brief contact had hurt. Then she was in place, the backs of her thighs resting against his, his chest curving like a warm, damp wall at her back. In spite of herself, she shivered. His breath feathered out against her ear in a silent laugh, but all he said was "Hmmm," in a tone of rueful agreement. For a moment both his arms encircled her as he gathered in the reins. Then his right arm dropped to his side and he clucked to the bay.

They started out slowly, the right foot of each rider resting on the filly's saddle.

She had to think of something to say. *Anything*. But she was too busy feeling to think. With each rocking stride of the bay, Jordan's left arm rubbed the side of her waist . . . a slow, tantalizing friction. His breath warmed the back of her neck. The blood was zinging through her veins, and ripples of sensation traveled up and down her legs everywhere they touched his. She shivered again.

"Cold?" he asked huskily, and his lips brushed her ear.

"No." If she'd been any warmer, she would have melted. "I'm fine."

"Finer than—" Whatever he'd meant to say, he checked himself. His right arm came around her, and his fingers spread gently against her stomach.

There was no doubt about it, she would melt. How could one feel so boneless and light at the same time? With a sigh of pure happiness she leaned against him, her back molding itself to his chest, and he breathed that silent rueful laugh again. "Oh, Kara," he muttered. His hand moved an inch up her stomach, then down again.

Then "All right," he said in a different tone of voice, as if he were consciously searching for a businesslike tone. "Bring your left leg over and hook it around the saddle horn, as if you were riding sidesaddle. I won't let you fall."

As she did so, his arm tightened around her. "I've never heard of breaking a horse like this before," she said breathlessly.

"Don't know anyone else who does it this way," he agreed. "But it works. She'll be too tired to fight you. And she can't hurt either herself or you out here. Worst case is you get a dunking, and even that's not likely."

They were nearing the downstream end of his exercise circuit. He turned the pair slowly, then said, "Okay, can you put a bit more weight on her?"

"Sure." Depending on his arm to steady her, she leaned out toward the filly. The white ears twitched in alarm and stayed back. Not in the angry position, just watchful and wary.

"We'll ride like this a ways," he murmured, his voice losing its instructor's edge again. "You can lean over and pet her, keep reminding her you're there. You don't want to come out of nowhere, when you climb on her."

Kara leaned out to stroke the filly, but in her mind, her hand moved over a different body. She had only tried champagne once or twice in her life, but it felt like this, she realized—happiness bubbling and fizzing inside her. She could have stayed like this, with Jordan's arms around her, for the rest of her life and asked for nothing more. "Your cast is gone," she said suddenly, looking at his rein arm.

"Had it taken off in Kentucky," he agreed. "It was just a fracture." Again his lips brushed her ear and seemed to linger.

It felt only natural to touch his arm, to run her fingertips from his elbow to his wide, bony wrist. "Looks all right. Does it feel okay?"

"Better than that." He laughed, with that queer, growling undertone to his laughter. "Are you doing this on purpose?"

"Doing what?" She turned to give him a wicked, gleaming smile over her shoulder. Treat her like a kid, would he? She'd show him yet.

His lips brushed the side of her jaw, then withdrew even as she sighed and closed her eyes. Arching her neck, she rested her head against his shoulder. He laughed aloud suddenly, but there was a trace of bitterness to the sound. "Damn it, Kara, will you cut this out!"

"Cut what out?" She laughed, opening her eyes.

He kissed the top of her head, but it was a rough kiss, full of exasperation as much as tenderness.

"Practicing on me, dammit! I'm not made of stone, you know." His fingers moved against her stomach again, then hardened and pressed into her softness. "Find somebody your own age to pick on, can't you?"

"That's what you want me to do?" she murmured, turning and trying to see his face.

But he wouldn't meet her eyes. He looked past her instead, the muscles in his jaw hardening.

"I'm not practicing," she said when he wouldn't answer. *It's just that I love you,* she thought fiercely. *That I want to be with you, to touch you, know you through and through.* But how could she say that? She couldn't.

"That's exactly what you're doing. You're too young to have a clue what you want," he growled, his lips at her ear.

She shivered and shook her head. "Jordan, I'm twenty, not twelve. That's plenty old enough to know what I want."

"Right," he said, but he meant exactly the opposite, the way he said it. "I know about twenty-year-olds, sweetheart. The one I married was twenty-one—straight out of college."

"And?" she said when he didn't go on.

"And twenty—or twenty-one—isn't ready for marriage. Not by a long shot. Hell, I was only twenty-two— I wasn't ready myself. No one is at that age. You have to sow your wild oats, have to knock around in this world, find out who you are, before you know who's right for you. I wouldn't marry a woman-child again for all the horses in Texas."

And that's what he thought she was. He was telling her so clearly. His hand moved up to her chin, and he turned her head back gently. He kissed the corner of her mouth, a rough, sweet kiss that was over before she could respond. "For luck, short stuff," he said. "Now get the heck out of ny lap and on that blasted filly where you belong, will you?''

Jordan hardly spoke at all while they broke the white filly. t was as if he regretted all he'd said and was now compen- ating for it. But Kara had much to think about.

She had to devote half her mind to the filly, soothing her onstantly with word and caress. And she had to watch out or her left leg—keep it forward so that it wasn't mashed between the two horses when the filly lunged. But Jordan vas right, she was too tired to fight much and could hardly buck at all with her halter rope snubbed tight. As the min- ites passed, the filly's leaps and halts smoothed out to a teady, slogging trot, and her ears began to relax. She swung ier nose to bump the bay's cheek. ''She's saying, 'so this is vhat it's all about, huh?''' Kara said, laughing.

''Could be,'' Jordan agreed and lapsed back into si- ence.

Kara stroked the filly's neck and imagined again that she vas stroking Jordan's thigh, which jogged only inches from ier hand. Her body still tingled all over as if his physical resence somehow changed the way the air pressed upon her body. She didn't know whether to feel blue or over the ainbow, his words had confused her as much as his body hrew her own into a confusion of ragged breathing and acing pulse. She thought they'd been talking about love, nd he'd talked about marriage.

But what had he been telling her? Could it be possible that : had ever crossed his mind—marriage? Marriage to her? But if that's what he meant, he'd also warned her that he ejected the notion out of hand.

Or had his words been a more general kind of warning, hat she was too young to become seriously involved with nyone, not just him?

I'm old enough to know what I want! She threw him a mutinous look, and he returned it with one that was warily neutral.

"You're doing fine," he said evenly. "You've got a nice seat. Did you ride mostly bareback?" When she nodded, he smiled for the first time. "Best training there is, for balance. Would you like to keep training her for me?"

She could feel her eyes opening wide as she nodded delightedly. Then she caught her breath. "But I— I couldn't do it in the daytime. The barn, you know. But early mornings? Or evenings?"

"Evenings, then," he agreed. "We'll do creek work for a few more days. We'll put her on a longer lead tomorrow, then within a couple of days, you'll be on your own."

Her smile was so brilliant that it won an answering one from him. "Does she have a name?" Kara asked, her hand on the filly's neck.

"She's a Smoky Joe filly out of Dream Chaser," Jordan said. "I call her Burning Dream."

CHAPTER NINE

"EVERYTHING'S SET UP," Kara declared as she stopped by Hank and checked her list again. "I've set out the nails, the hammers, the mallets, the anchor pikes. The temporary braces are right where we'll need them. How are you coming?"

Hank moved the big pulley block that he'd tied to the cross beam. "I'm about set." He turned to squint anxiously at the gin pole that loomed overhead. It would serve as a primitive sort of crane. "We won't know for sure till we start to lift this, whether I've got her dead center. If she's off balance, we'll set her back down and move the ropes till she is."

Kara also tipped her head to study the gin pole. It was simply a tree trunk, some thirty-five feet high. Three ropes held it upright—one rope stretched to a nearby oak tree, one went to the stack of timbers that would be used later in the building. The third was tied to the axle of Mike Cavazos's truck, lent to them specially for this occasion.

At the top of the gin pole a large block and tackle was attached to a forked limb and connected by a big nylon line to the pulley at the cross beam of the bent. The line made a few more turns for mechanical advantage and led finally to the winch on Chris's Jeep, which was parked at the edge of the foundation.

It was the winch that would provide the power to raise the bent. And then once it was upright and had dropped into its

slots in the foundation, they'd nail on some temporary di
agonal bracing to make it stay while they raised the othe
four frames.

Kara found that she was shaking slightly with excite
ment. It sounded so easy when you said it, but to actuall
do it! The bents seemed too heavy to ever leave the ground
She wasn't quite sure how to use her anchor pike yet, an
they were going to have an audience on top of it all. It wa
a Sunday, and she didn't think one of Jordan's men mean
to miss the occasion. Even as she thought it, a pickup ap
peared over the rise from the direction of the bunkhouse
It's rear bed was packed tight with whooping men. Mor
perched on the railing, hanging on to each other every tim
the truck hit a bump.

"You're sure you don't want them to help?" she asked
nodding at the exuberant bunch.

Hank snorted. "They'd just get in the way. We've got a
the help we need already."

And he also wanted to prove something to Jordan, Kar
suspected secretly. The two of them had had it out yester
day, while she was off fetching lunch from their apartmen
in the foaling barn. She'd come back in time to catch the en
of the confrontation, to see both of them looking as stif
necked as a couple of sparring roosters. But somehow Hanl
had won this round. Jordan hadn't been able to deny tha
they'd done a splendid job so far. He'd tried to order Han
to use his men for the actual lifting, but Hank had insiste
that it was safer without the confusion of too many help
ers; that he was darned if he'd be responsible for the pro
ject if he couldn't choose his own crew.

Teeth clenched, Jordan had exacted a promise that the
wouldn't start the raising until he was on-site. And hi
parting shot was that he'd stop the work in an instant if h
decided anyone was at risk.

"Okay!" Chris Haley whooped as he swung down from he back of the pickup. "Let's get this show on the road!"

But not without Jordan, Kara thought nervously. She urned to look up the hill toward the big house. Surely he wouldn't make them all wait? That would hurt Hank's pride or sure, if the men realized he had to wait for Jordan's supervision. But even as she worried, she saw his long-legged orm striding down the hill.

She'd found more frustration than satisfaction, riding in Jordan's company these past few days. He was keeping her at a very careful arm's length, hardly looking at her at all, imiting their conversation strictly to horse talk. Only once had she surprised any kind of warmer reaction from him, when Dream had thrown her on the third day of training. The temper tantrum had happened in the shallows of the reek, and she had come up soaked and laughing, to find Jordan swinging off his bay with a look of almost frightening intensity. But it had changed almost immediately to amusement when he realized she was all right. And by the ime he'd returned from capturing Dream for her, even that ad faded to his usual expression of aloofness.

Still, aloof or not, there was no one in the world she'd rather be with than Jordan Stonehall. "Morning!" she alled as she hurried to meet him.

"Kara, make him take some help," he said, cutting traight to the matter at hand. He kept on walking and she ell into step.

But this was way too late to change Hank's mind. "I can't make Dad do anything he doesn't want to do, Jordan."

"Oh, really?" he muttered. "I thought you were the Tate who called the shots. I figured you tied his shoelaces for im, when he needed it."

"Dad is perfectly able to take care of himself," she said oldly.

"My point exactly," he growled. "So what are you doing, hanging around with him at twenty? Most people grow up move out."

Hank had needed her help. But this was no time to try to explain, with Jordan in this kind of mood. What was eating him this morning? "Which am I, Jordan?" she asked instead. "A domineering little shrew who calls all the shots, or a child who's afraid to leave the nest?"

"Why can't you be both?" he asked with insulting pleasantness.

It was almost as if he was trying to dislike her. She shot him a furious look, then angled away from him to join Chris and Hank. Her hands were clenched so hard, the nails bit into her palms.

But if it was difficult to get along with a certain rock headed Texan, it was easy to build barns, Kara decided an hour later. Wiping her sweating face, she stepped back from the first bent, and stood staring up at it, the men's rowdy applause ringing in her ears. The raising had gone as smooth as silk. She turned to grin at her father, but he was simply standing by his post, one hand caressing the wood while he stared at the outline of his barn traced against the sky.

Instead she hurried over to Chris, who had handled the winch for them, easing the bent off the ground with a slow steady pull that had made the task easy. "What a job!" she said grinning at him. "Thank you!"

He caught her in a swift bear hug. "*Hooeee!* I love this I'm gonna build me a house for sure! What a piece of cake."

"We've still got four frames to go," she warned him "Better not say anything yet!" As she disengaged herself from his friendly embrace, her eyes met Jordan's across the foundation. He stood by Mike Cavazos. The foreman was talking and gesturing enthusiastically at the barn, but that black look on Jordan's face was for Kara alone.

You wanted me to practice on someone my age, didn't you? she thought angrily, as she hurried off to join her father.

As the sun climbed the sky, the barn rose to meet it. The second bent went easily, except for a minor problem when one tenon proved to be too wide for its mortise. But Chris was able to hold the bent upright while Hank shaved a quarter inch off the offending peg, and it dropped into place as smooth as you please.

After that, around one in the afternoon, there was a pause. The gin pole had to be moved to get the proper angle between it and the bent for the end wall. Once it was in position, the end frame went up like a dream, though Kara's arms were beginning to ache with the effort of holding the big anchor pike.

It was her job—and Hank's at the other post—to jam the anchor pike into the mortise to prevent any sliding. Then once the bent was almost to the vertical, the pike had to be pulled out at the last second so that the tenon could drop into its mortise hole.

She finished nailing the diagonal braces into place and set her hammer down. Now they would have to move the gin pole again, to raise the final two bents at the other end of the barn. She let out a weary sigh, and rolled her aching shoulders, then looked up to find Jordan watching from a distance, his dark brows pulled together in a frown.

He probably didn't approve of seeing a woman sweat, she thought, and lifted her chin defiantly. It was odd how that electric awareness, that *connection* between them held just as fast in anger as it did in happiness. *Can't you feel that?* she begged him silently, then turned away, suddenly ashamed. Why was she pining after a man who didn't want her?

She found that Mrs. Cavazos had driven a card table and a picnic lunch down from the big house, for all to share. As Kara made herself a ham sandwich she shot a suspicious glance at Jordan. Had he asked his housekeeper to provide this bounty, or had it been her own idea? But for once Jordan wasn't waiting to meet her questioning gaze. He was wandering among the bents, staring at the evolving shape of the barn.

At the far side of the foundation, Hank was doing the same thing, a look of so much joy on his face that Kara was suddenly frightened for him. They weren't done yet. It was too soon to exult. She walked over and knocked on the middle bent.

"Superstitious?" Chris asked beside her.

She laughed and shrugged it away. "Just trying to believe it's really up there! I can hardly believe it."

"Just two frames to go," Chris drawled comfortably. They sat down on the sill next to Mike Cavazos and rested their paper plates in their laps. Kara took a forkful of the potato salad, then stopped, fork halfway to her mouth. Tail held high and prim, a sleek tiger cat was parading across the barnyard toward her, two tiger kittens tumbling at her heels. "Oh, my gosh!" croaked Kara. She looked around wildly. Had Hank seen them?

"What's the matter, don't you like cats?" Chris asked. He held out a chunk of ham to the cat. She sniffed it with grand disdain, then, once he'd set it at his feet, she gobbled it up and looked around for more.

"It's just *that* cat," Kara said weakly.

"*You!*" Hank exclaimed, coming up behind them. "What do you think you're doing here?"

The cat blinked her golden eyes at him, then leaped gracefully to the sill and down again to his feet. She rubbed herself on his shins.

"Get away from me, you she-devil!" Hank danced back a step, but the cat followed. "Now stop that!"

"Hey," Chris laughed. "That's just ol' Creampuff. She's friendly."

"*Too* damn friendly!" Hank stepped hurriedly over the sill and found himself facing the two tiger puffballs she'd left behind. "I give up," he groaned. "We might as well quit for the day."

Kara handed him her plate. "Have half my sandwich, Dad, and don't worry."

"Don't worry! With this crowd around? We've been hexed!"

"Maybe they came to apologize," Kara said soothingly. She pinched a bit of ham off her sandwich and offered it to one of the kittens. "My," she cooed to it. "How you have grown!"

"Yeah, they're growing like a couple of houses afire," Chris agreed. "They've been mooching around the bunk-house, the last couple weeks. Eat anything that moves, just 'bout."

Hank put his half of his sandwich back on her plate uneaten. "I feel sick." He scowled at the cats.

But if anything, the cats' coming was a good omen, Kara decided. The fourth bent went up in record time. And once it was raised, the bolder of the two kittens stormed it and climbed halfway to the cross beams, to the cheers and laughter of all present. Even Hank looked a bit mollified.

"Just one to go," he said, comforting Kara. "You holding up all right, honey?"

"I'm fine, Dad." But tonight she would feel as if she'd been run down by a herd of elephants. She plucked the kitten off the post and set it on her shoulder, where it purred like the winch on Chris's Jeep.

The kitten sat on her shoulder while the final bent rose slowly toward the sky. Levering her anchor pike against the post, which was trying to slide toward her, Kara groaned aloud with the effort. *Just this one more.* Looking at at the Jeep, she met Chris's cheerful gaze, then saw Jordan standing just beyond. He frowned, took a step toward her, and she shook her head. She was darned if she was going to take his help now. This was going to be her and Hank's victory, all the way. As the bent shifted, the kitten gathered itself, wriggling its rear end, and leaped to the rising post.

And from somewhere behind and above, a sharp *crack* rang out.

"Run!" someone yelled as the frame started to fall. It stopped with a groaning jolt, and Kara turned to see Hank jamming a brace into place between the ground and his post, fighting to keep it upright. But it was too late to brace her side. Kara leaped for the kitten as the bent sagged to her unsupported side and toppled again. Her hand closed on soft fur, then something crashed into her with the momentum of a freight train.

As she went flying, all breath knocked out of her, she saw the second bent fall—half a ton of wood, scything a majestic arc between her and the sky, to the groan of crackling wood. Then she hit the ground, something smashed down on her, and the lights went out.

"Kara, baby, speak to me!" Hank's voice begged beyond the darkness.

"Move her and I'll kill you, Tate," a deeper voice snarled. "If her back's hurt . . ."

"If her back's hurt, it's because you tackled her, you big idiot!"

"If she's hurt, it's your fool pride that hurt her! If you'd accepted some help—"

"From the likes of you? We were doing just fine till the block broke."

"Exactly."

Jordan's cool, dry hand cupped her cheek. At his touch, she opened her eyes to a ring of staring faces and a sky too bright to be borne. She closed them again. "I'm . . . not hurt." Her breath was coming back now—she must have fainted. "Where's the kitten?"

"Headed for the hills the minute it landed," Jordan growled. "If you'd run, yourself, instead of worrying about a worthless cat— Are you all right?"

"Yes." She opened her eyes again and tried to sit up.

But his hands closed on her shoulders. "Not till I'm sure."

"Not till *I'm* sure, you mean! Now get out of the way and let me take care of my own." Hank looked as if he meant to push Jordan aside.

Jordan's brows drew together dangerously, but he let go of Kara. "Then do a better job of it!" He stood stiffly and glared at the two of them. "Don't move her till you're sure her spine's all right." He turned and stalked away.

By the time Kara had satisfied Hank and Chris that she could move each limb without pain, and that her back felt just fine, that all she was, was bruised and sore, Jordan was gone.

Where had he gone? she wondered while she patiently repeated again and again the assurance that she was just fine, thank you, to each ranch hand who wanted to know.

Eventually they let her rise and move to a seat on the foundation sill, from where she could view the disaster.

The weight of the first bent had brought the second one crashing down with it. It was the second one that would have killed her but for Jordan. She shivered and looked around, wanting him there. His tackle had carried her and him and the kitten right under that falling guillotine. They had landed at almost mid-foundation, in a window of space created by the openess of the wood framework. If they'd landed three feet to either side... She shivered again.

Not long after that, Hank insisted that Kara go back to their apartment for a rest. Still dazed and sore, she went willingly, driven by Chris and Lew in a pickup. "This calls for a serious wake," Lew announced as she climbed from the truck. "Want to drive into town, Chris? We're gonna need supplies."

Chris shook his head and looked out the truck window at her, his blue eyes worried. "Sure you don't want a hand up the stairs, Kara?"

"I'm sure." At least not from Chris, sweet as he was.

After a long, hot shower, her bunk bed looked too good to resist. She lay down for just a minute, and the next time she opened her eyes, it was dark. She dressed slowly—her body had stiffened while she slept—then went in search of Hank. And Jordan, where was he?

Lew had suggested a wake, and that was just what they were giving the barn, Kara discovered when she reached the building site. A bonfire burned merrily. The Stonehall ranch hands sat on the remains of the fallen bents, their voices loud and cheerful. On the ground, a pile of empty Lone Star beer bottles caught the light, showing Kara some of the reason for their good humor. Mrs. Cavazos's card table was still in place, but now it held a clutter of uncooked hot dogs, buns, bags of potato chips and condiments. And, her eyes fixed on two bottles. *Bourbon.*

Swinging around, she found Hank seated at the center of a knot of men, Chris Haley's arm thrown over his shoulders. Chris bawled something in his ear and laughed at his joke himself. Hank only smiled weakly.

"Kara, I'm glad you came." Mike Cavazos appeared at her shoulder, carrying a stick on which a half dozen roasted hotdogs had been skewered. "You gotta talk to your dad, Kara. He's lower than a snake's knees. Keeps saying he almost killed you."

"That's silly!" Kara exclaimed. There was no way Hank could have predicted that accident. All the same, she should have anticipated this reaction. But was he drinking to overcome his guilt? She looked anxiously at the ranch foreman, but Mike smelt only faintly of beer— Jordan's right-hand man was expected to set an example for the others. And she knew that if the ranch hands themselves wanted to really tie one on, they'd do well to do it in town—not on Stonehall property. But Hank— Hank had promised Jordan he'd stay bone dry, till the project was done.

"Hey, there she is!" Chris yelled.

Kara turned, and a ragged cheer went up. Everyone was grinning at her. Embarrassed, she smiled and gave them a big "Howdy!" wave.

"Let's have a toast!" Chris yelled, lifting the bottle of Jack Daniels he held. He reached across the circle to slop liquor into the paper cup that Lew was holding two-handed. Then he grabbed the can of pop that Hank held and poured bourbon into it till it ran down the sides of the can. Chris raised his bottle, and the others raised their drinks. "To the pretty lady—a pretty lucky lady!"

Don't drink that, Dad, Kara thought, her eyes fixed on her father's.

Can still raised in salute, Hank smiled at her, a shaky, wavering smile. "And to the best partner a man ever had..."

"Tate." Jordan's voice rang out, sounding overloud in the sudden silence.

"Uh-oh!" someone murmured. Another ranch hand rose quickly and left the circle.

The rancher stepped into the firelight. "That's the last straw."

Oh, lord, so he had seen Chris pour the liquor. Kara stepped forward, hand outstretched.

"This?" Hank looked from Jordan to the can he held and back to the rancher.

"That," Jordan growled as he stalked closer. "That's what got you into trouble in the first place. We had an agreement."

"So we did," Hank agreed with a rusty laugh. He tossed the can at Jordan's boots. Chris Haley and another hand stood and staggered away into the darkness.

Jordan didn't bother to look down. "Pack your bags and get out."

"*Jordan!*" Kara rushed him, not knowing what she'd do when she arrived, wanting to push the words back into his mouth—to undo them. "You don't mean it!"

"Kara, stay out of this!" He caught her shoulders and shook her. "For once in your life let your dad fight his own fight."

"Don't you tell my daughter what to do!" Hank cocked his fists and bore down on them, his bald head gleaming in the firelight. "Get your hands off her."

"Dad, stop it!" Kara wrenched away from Jordan's grasp to plant her hands on her father's chest. His momentum knocked her backward into Jordan, who simply grabbed her arms and set her to one side.

"Get off my land," he grated, looking down at Hank. "The deal's off. Consider the debt settled. Just get the *hell* off my land before you kill that daughter you're so proud of, or somebody else."

"But what about the barn?" Kara cried.

He didn't look at her. "I'll get someone to finish it. A professional this time."

"Professional!" Hank swung a roundhouse punch, then staggered as Jordan simply stepped back from it.

"That's right," the rancher said coolly. "Someone who stays sober on the job and builds with his head, not his pride. We're lucky we didn't lose somebody today."

"Lose somebody! Tell *me* about losing! I always lose when I mess with a lying, cheating Stonehall. I should have had my head examined, getting into this deal!" Hank threw another punch, and again Jordan simply backed away from it. "Stand still and *fight*, you cheater!"

Kara looked around wildly. Someone had to help her separate them. But everyone had vanished, even Mike Cavazos, whether to save Hank's pride, or to duck trouble, she couldn't say.

"Nobody calls me a cheater," Jordan snarled. "If you were thirty years younger, you old coot—"

"*I'll* call you a cheater. Who blinded my horse—tell me that? If that isn't cheating! You blinded Joe so I'd sell him back to you, didn't you? That day I let you go in his stall...."

Jordan stopped stone still, his mouth ajar, eyes widening. Hank's punch thumped his ribs solidly, rocking him back a step. The rancher threw up his hands and clenched them.

"*Jordan!*" Kara flung her arms around Hank from behind and hung on. "Don't you dare!"

"Then get him out of my sight!" Jordan roared. "*Now!* Blind a horse? Get him the *hell* off my land!" Jordan backed away from Hank's flailing fists, then swung around and retreated into the darkness. He stopped and spun back, pointing his finger at her. "Tonight, Kara!"

Tears dripping down her face, she stared after him till his shadow was one with the blackness and she could no longer hear his footsteps over Hank's panting. Finally she let Hank go. "Well...guess that's that, Dad," she said drearily. More tears dripped, and she wiped them aside. Hank wouldn't turn to face her, but his own arm rose, and he swiped his forearm across his eyes.

"Yeah..." he murmured. He tried to laugh, but it came out more like a bear snuffling. "Yeah. Damn bad-luck barn..."

What had Jordan said once, that he looked for excuses, not solutions? That hadn't been fair, but it was that memory that made her say, "If you hadn't drunk—" Then she bit her tongue. Now was no time for reproaches.

Hank laughed that soggy laugh again. "That's the worst of it. I ain't had anything but soda pop tonight."

She caught his arm and pulled him around. "But I saw Chris— And I think Jordan did, too."

"They were toasting you, baby. What was I supposed to do, not lift my glass? But I wasn't going to drink it. I'd given him my word."

With a little groan of despair, Kara hugged him. It had all been his foolish, stiff-necked pride. "Oh, Daddy..." For just a second, she thought of running up to the big house, telling this to Jordan.

But no, the fight had gone past that. There was no going back, not after Hank had accused him of blinding Smoky Joe. Tucking her fingers around his arm, she tugged her dad gently toward the foaling barn. "Guess we better go pack."

CHAPTER TEN

A MOCKINGBIRD warbled a one-bird symphony, welcoming a sun that wouldn't peek above the hills for hours yet. Kara trudged out from under the oaks and stood looking at the skeleton of the barn, a mug of coffee steaming in her hand. Absently she lifted it, sipped, then drifted closer.

Mike Cavazos had driven Hank into town the night before, to sleep at a friend's house until they could sort themselves out. Kara had stayed behind. They'd both been too exhausted, body and heart, to pack up their tools. So she had sent Hank ahead with the promise that she would follow with their gear in the morning. And then she had spent her last night in the groom's apartment in the foaling barn. Not sleeping.

She sank down on the foundation and took another sip of coffee, then looked at the three bents they'd raised. They'd come so close. You could see already the final shape of the barn. But now it was over, Hank's dream.

And hers. Tears burning behind her lashes, she ducked her head and drank again. She hadn't slept at all. Jordan's face, Jordan's hands, Jordan's voice had haunted her all night long. It was over. He was sending her away without a pang of regret or a second thought. All those silly dreams she'd cherished.... She shook her head bitterly. *Forget it. It's over. It never even was, except in your head.*

She stood and walked to the fallen bents. Sipping coffee, she stared down at them dully, no longer hearing the bird's

celebration. The end bent had fallen without breaking itself, as far as she could see. The bent that Jordan had saved
her from had cracked its tenons off when it fell.

That one would have to be rebuilt. But it would not be
such a big job. She and Hank could have done it in half a
day.

Could have. She grimaced and looked at the framework
again. Why was she feeling sorry for herself, when Hank
had lost *this*? She mourned something that had never really
existed, but Hank— Hank had seen his dream rise here once
before. He'd needed to rebuild it. Needed to believe that he
could change his luck. That he still had the old magic in his
hands and his head, and that he could make that magic rise
up in wood.

That's what Jordan had taken away from her father.

She stopped, coffee mug at her lips, then shook her head.
All right, Jordan, that wasn't fair, she admitted. She
wouldn't make excuses. She would look the truth in the eye,
even when it hurt. Hank had ended his own dream last night
with his own foolish words. If he hadn't accused Jordan like
that, they could have worked something out.

But not now. Jordan had meant what he'd said, when
he'd ordered Hank off his land.

The mocker sailed out of the nearest oak and landed,
wings fluttering, on the middle bent. Tipping back its gray
head, it trilled a jubilant improvisation on its theme. Kara
stared blindly at the bird, Jordan's words echoing in her
head. He'd ordered *Hank* off his land. He'd said nothing
about her going! The faintest stirring of hope moved
through her heart like a few notes of bird song. Could that
mean that he wanted her to stay? But immediately she
shrugged the thought off. No, hopes hurt too much when
you found out you were wrong. She wasn't going to be that
foolish again. But still, he'd left her a loophole.

And this barn needed to be built—had to be built! Hank and she had planned to carve their names and the date on the plate beam in the loft, where the original date had been carved. She looked around, her eyes sweeping the neat stacks of lumber. The girts, the big horizontal beams that would tie each bent to its neighbor were cut already. And so were the mortises. If she were to finish the barn herself, it would still be half Hank's.

He'd said it himself—that once all the bents were raised the rest of the work would be downhill. If she finished the barn, she could still carve both their names in it. Even if Hank never set foot on Stonehall land again, he could get on with his life, if he knew that the barn stood there with his name on it for the next hundred years.

Heart thundering, she looked around again. She'd have to make a start, a damned good start before Jordan found her. And when he did? She wouldn't let herself think about that. She'd face that fight when it came.

First you have to drag the broken bent out of the way, she told herself. And Chris's Jeep stood waiting. Putting the coffee mug down on the foundation, Kara rolled up her sleeves. She could do this. Would do it. And there wasn't man born of woman that would stop her.

By the time Mrs. Cavazos drove down to clean up the remains of the ranch hands' wake, Kara had disassembled the broken bent and moved its timbers to one side. Using the jacks, the rollers and the Jeep, she had dragged the undamaged frame she meant to raise into position, ready to be lifted. She'd found a block to replace the one that had failed yesterday, and was puzzling how to get it to the top of the gin pole.

"The señor knows you do this?" Mrs. Cavazos asked doubtfully, as Kara rolled one of the steel drums to the base of the gin pole.

"Not yet," she panted. She sat down on the roller and looked at the older woman. "And would you please, please not tell him, Mrs. Cavazos? I know he'll find out, but I'd rather tell him myself, if you don't mind."

Frowning, the housekeeper shook her head and clucked her tongue. Then she shrugged, an expansive shrug for such a tiny woman. "And how can I? The señor is gone to the hospital. By the time he comes back, well, this day I shop, go to Kerrville, and then I visit my sister."

"He's at the hospital?" Her heartbeat quickening, Kara spread her hands flat against the cool steel of the drum.

"The arm. He hurt it again. You did not know?"

That flying tackle. He must have caught his weight on it as they landed. Kara bit her lip. "No... well, anyway, thanks, Mrs. Cavazos."

The woman shrugged. "It is nothing. And now I must hurry."

Kara hurried, too. Once she brought the gin pole down, it took no time to tie on the new block and reload its ropes.

Raising the gin pole took some thought, but she'd learned much from Hank about mechanical leverage, these past few weeks. With the Jeep supplying the pull power, she got it back up.

And somehow she raised the bent as well. It took her all afternoon, devising ways to replace the two men she was missing from her raising team. But she was learning that almost anything could be done, given the will—and a lot of luck.

When Mike Cavazos finally rode by, he found her bracing the bent posts. "Kara, are you crazy?" He stared up at the bent. "I thought someone had taken you into town. What the blue blazes do you think you're doing?"

"Raising a barn," she told him around a mouthful of nails. "Do you think you could help me lift that other brace?" She was staggeringly tired by now. To her aching arms, the fifty-pound timbers weighed a ton apiece.

"It's as good as my job!" he muttered, but with a quick glance in the direction of the distant big house, he swung the wood up into place for her. Rapidly he set up the other temporary braces, then watched her with a worried frown in place of his usual smile. "After you've done that, Kara, I've got to stop you. If the boss knew you were doing this..."

"Leave the boss to me," she said, crouching to nail the foot of the brace to the sill.

"Kara, I'm foreman. I'm paid to know what the boss wants before he does, and to see that it's done. And I know he wouldn't want you doing this. It's dangerous—you saw that yourself yesterday."

"Mike, I'm sorry." She patted his boot tip and scrambled around to the other side of the bent to toenail the second brace. "But I'm not stopping."

"All right then, Kara." When he rode off, he was headed toward the main house.

She was nailing the final brace when she heard a car coming fast. She looked up to see what she'd dreaded—the Jag bouncing down the hill. A cloud of dust rose as Jordan stomped on the brakes and swung out of the car. *"Kara!"* he bellowed, as his feet hit the ground.

Clenching her teeth, she set the final nail into position and swung the hammer. She was shaking so hard she missed it. She aimed more carefully and hit it a good one—got in one more lick, then his hand closed on her wrist, and he pulled the hammer out of her grasp.

"What the hell do you think you're doing?" He tossed the hammer over his shoulder.

"Following through." She leaned against the post to look up at him. "We told you we'd build you a barn."

"And I told you the debt was settled. Forget about it."

"Can't do that," she murmured. No more than she'd eve
be able to forget this man. His tawny hair was tousled, as i
Mike had awakened him from sleep, or he'd been runnin,
his hands through it in a fury. His left arm was back in
cast. Tiredly, she touched it. "You okay?"

"Recracked it, and don't change the subject. Kara, yo
can't do this."

"I'm doing it." She gestured at the bent overhead. "Onl
one to go."

"And that's how we leave it, you little lunatic. No more
It's over."

"You owe me," she said, lifting her chin.

"Ho, no!" He laughed under his breath. Catching he
arm, he drew her closer. "You've tried that one, one tim
too many, sweetheart. It won't work anymore. I paid tha
debt off yesterday. A life for a life, that's fair and square."

And with that debt canceled, her last hold over him, thei
last connection, was broken. She hadn't thought... Couldn'
think now, was too tired to. All she could do was blink bacl
the tears.

His hand tightened on her arm. "It's over, short stuff,"
he said gruffly. "Let's pack your tools and I'll drive you int
town."

It was over. It had never been, if he could not only sen
her away, but could take her and dump her like an un
wanted cat. But there was still Hank. Still this barn. He
eyes filling and overflowing, she shook her head. "I'm no
going! You can't make me go. I've got a barn to build."

"Kara!" His breath hissed between his teeth. "Don't b
a fool. You'd kill yourself trying to build this. It can't b
done."

Her voice squeaked dangerously close to hysteria. "It *ca*
be done. I'm *doing* it. I did it today, and I'm going to keep
on doing it till it's done. I keep my word even if you don't."

"You and your idiotic pride!" He caught her shoulders as she turned away and swung her around to face him.

"What's wrong with pride?" she sobbed, struggling to wrench free. "That's all some people have left, didn't you know?" She shoved his chest, then hammered on him when still he held her. "Now let *go* of me! You aren't driving me anywhere. You try and drive me, and I'll fight you every inch of the way, so help me! I'm *staying*!" Her hands flattened against his chest as he yanked her too close to hit him again. "I'm staying—" she sobbed, and then his mouth muffled anything else she might have cried.

For just a moment she fought him, her eyes widening with the shock of the caress. Then, with a moan, she arched her body to meet his, and her head tipped back. His arms tightened to support her yielding weight as his kiss gentled and deepened. Lashes fluttering closed, she retreated into darkness, shutting out everything in the world but the strength of his arms, their hearts' rushing clamor, the thrust and caress of tongue meeting tongue. The essential, overpowering rightness of this. Exhaustion gave way to an aching, honeyed warmth that radiated from deep within.

And then it was over. She smiled shakily, blindly, as his lips roved across her cheek, her eyelashes, and through the hair at her temple. "Little lunatic," he growled in her ear.

"I'm staying," she whispered, leaning her forehead against his shoulder. And she wasn't just talking about barns now.

"We'll see," he said in a queer husky voice, and brushed his cheek across the top of her head.

Slowly her smile faded against his shirt. *We'll see?* He didn't know now? Couldn't feel it? The warmth faded, leaving nothing behind but a leaden exhaustion. Then nothing had been settled for him as it had for her with that kiss. A desolate sigh of defeat escaped her. She was doing it again, wasn't she? Mistaking his simple male pleasure in holding a warm and willing woman with something more. Something lasting.

"There's something I need to know," Jordan said. His hands slid to her arms, and he held her out from him. "What your dad said last night, about my blinding Joe... Do you believe that?"

She felt his fingers tighten on her shoulders while she considered it. Had she ever thought so, even years ago? Perhaps back then she'd wondered... But knowing him now... Slowly she shook her head. "No. No, I don't believe it." As his hands and the hard line of his mouth relaxed, she added, "And I don't think Dad does either, really. He was just so mad last night, and when he's mad, he... says things."

But his face had hardened. "There are some things you don't say, Kara. Not if you have an ounce of sense in your head."

"He does, it's just that—"

"Look." He cut her off. "It's not worth arguing about. I don't want to argue at all tonight, and you're too tired to hold up your end if we did."

He had that right. She found herself being led to his Jag and driven to the foaling barn. When she realized that his intention was to collect her clothes and move her up to the big house, she had no energy left to fight him. Especially now after he pointed out that she could take a hot tub bath there, as opposed to a shower in the groom's quarters.

They entered the main house from a cobblestoned court yard at the rear. Carrying her suitcase, he led her in through the kitchen.

Mrs. Cavazos rushed at them, a carrot she'd been cutting in one hand, a large chef's knife upheld for emphasis in the other. "You have guests, señor! *Alla* on the patio." Sh jerked her chin fiercely at the verandah that the L-shaped house half enclosed.

"The Dickersons?" Jordan swore under his breath. "They weren't due until tomorrow, Mrs. Cavazos."

"This I know!" She turned back to her cutting board and chopped off the end of the carrot with a vicious whack.

"Mrs. Cavazos?" a woman's voice called sweetly. The door leading from kitchen to verandah opened. "Might we have one more pitcher of those *delicious* daiquir—" As the woman's dark head appeared around the door, her beautiful mouth shaped an O of delighted surprise. "Why, Jordan! There you are." The brunette hurtled across the room to throw her arms around him. "I know we're a day early, but Houston was just *so* boring." She kissed his cheek smartly. "I hope you don't mind."

"Not at all, Sabrina," Jordan said. As the woman backed away a step, his eyes moved from her to Kara and back again.

It took no mind reader to know what he was thinking. The contrast between her and the sleek brunette was so brutal, Kara would have sunk through the red tiles underfoot if she could have done so. This was the type of woman she'd always pictured for Jordan, with her simple silk dress that whispered softly of money and taste, the rubies in her ears, that unshakable self-assurance that came of education and wealth and opportunity. This was someone from Jordan's world, offering her slender, manicured hand to Kara's dust-smudged fingers with only the tiniest hesitation, while Jordan made the introduction. Her green eyes moved over Kara's work clothes and a face that Kara suddenly realized must be tear-stained, with an expression of cool, but friendly, puzzlement.

And then Kara had to go through it all again, as Sabrina Dickerson's brother strolled in from the verandah. He was older than Sabrina, perhaps thirty-five to her thirty, and clearly a close friend of Jordan's. "Hello, hello," he said warmly as he took Kara's hand, but his keen eyes measured her and came away with a hint of ironic amusement in their depths.

And why should he not be amused? She was so clearly out of place here. Too young, too unsophisticated, far, far too grubby after a hard day's work on the barn. It was what Jordan had been trying to tell her all along, wasn't it? That she would never measure up?

And then the ordeal was over. Refusing Jordan's suggestion that she join them for dinner in town, she retreated behind the rigid back of Mrs. Cavazos to the guest room. With a sob of relief, she headed straight for the connecting bathroom and stripped off her clothes. But it would take more than soap to wash away the humiliation of that encounter.

She was chin-deep in bubbles when the knock came on the outer door. Sinking lower in the water, Kara rested her head against the rim of the tub and did not answer. Let whoever it was think she'd gone to sleep.

Instead the outer door opened. "Kara?" Jordan called from the bedroom.

She half sat up with a splash, realizing she'd left the bathroom door open, then hastily subsided into the bubbles.

"Kara?" Jordan stopped outside the door. "Are you all right?"

"I'm fine—don't come in!" she called. "I'm in the tub."

He laughed softly. "What's that perfume? Bubble bath?"

"Yes," she muttered.

"This I've got to see," he said and swung into the doorway. Lounging against the door frame, he smiled and shook his head.

"Out!" she said between her teeth.

Instead he sauntered forward and sat on the edge of the tub. "I brought you this." He held out a cocktail glass, filled with a bright pink icy foam. "Strawberry daiquiri. I think you deserve one."

Unwillingly she lifted an arm out of the bubbles to take the glass and saw his eyes darken as she did so. She sipped the daiquiri consideringly, never having tried one before. His eyes lingered on her lips as she licked the ice off them and sighed. "It's gorgeous. Now go away?"

Instead he reached to run a knuckle along her cheek, brushing a poof of foam off her wet skin. "Come into town with us," he countered. "I can't ask Mrs. Cavazos to cook tonight. She'd poison me for sure."

"No, thanks." Closing her eyes, she took another sip of the drink.

He gave a little wordless growl of exasperation. "I can't neglect John Dickerson, Kara. He's a bloodstock agent. I mean to sell him two or three brood mares, and a colt or two."

"And his sister?" she murmured.

"She's just along for the ride."

Sabrina was along for Jordan, Kara knew instinctively. But there was nothing she could do about that. She was what she was, and Jordan had told her in a hundred ways it was not what he wanted. Then he'd proved it, by wanting to send her away tonight. She sighed again, then started as he lifted the drink out of her hand. She opened her eyes to find him sipping from her glass.

"Not bad," he agreed and set the glass on the edge of the tub. "Well, you're sure you won't join us?" When she nodded her head, he went on. "Then feel free to raid the fridge. I told Mrs. Cavazos to take the night off, so you've got the house to yourself." Reaching down, he scooped up a dollop of foam and dabbed it on the end of her nose. "Have fun," he said softly and left the room.

KARA HAD no desire to see what the lovely Sabrina Dickerson wore to breakfast. She had no doubt at all that whatever it was, it would outclass her work shirt and painter's pants. So she was out of the house before six, a chunk of bread and cheese in one hand, a coffee mug in the other as she hurried down the hill.

But if she had no hope left where Jordan was concerned, she still had a barn to build. She'd phoned Hank from the big house last night, after Jordan and his guests left for town. Her father had been no happier than Jordan at her tackling the project by herself. And she'd given him much the same answer. She'd set her heart on it. Nobody was going to stop her. "I'll be calling you, Dad," she'd promised. "I don't know what to do after the girts, so think about it. You're going to have to coach me over the phone." She'd called a loud goodbye over his squawk of protest, then hung up before they started quarreling.

When the Jaguar purred down the hill around ten, she was working furiously, chiseling a tenon into the end of one of the replacement posts for the broken bent. She looked up to see Jordan and the two Dickersons watching her through the windshield. She threw them a cheery wave and went right on working. But the driver's door opened, and Jordan unwound his lean height. His face wasn't cheerful at all. "What do I have to do to make you stop this, Kara?" he asked. "Tie you to a bed?"

"Why don't you leave me alone? I'm doing fine." She shaved another curl of yellow pine off the peg.

"So help me, I don't want to embarrass you in front of my guests, Kara, but—you're *not* raising this bent alone."

"No, I'm not," she agreed sweetly. "If I can finish it by noon, Chris promised me he'd help me on his lunch hour."

"*Haley . . .*" He almost spat the name out. She nodded agreement and didn't spare him another glance. After a few minutes of dour watching, he left her, and the car rolled off toward the stables.

But it returned at noon. This time when Jordan stepped from it, he was dressed in work jeans. Chris looked over Kara's shoulder and muttered, "*Uh* oh!"

She glanced up at the cowboy's worried face, then put a hand on his arm. "Leave him to me, Chris." She was darned if she'd let Jordan penalize Chris for helping her.

But though he shot Chris a bitter look, all Jordan said was, "Need a hand?"

Which was all he had to lend, Kara realized ruefully, as the bent went up. He shouldn't be helping her, with that fractured arm. But he stood at the far post, his anchor pike braced with his good hand and a foot, his gray eyes intent on the rising bent. On the winch, Chris was slow and cautious. Once the tenons had dropped into their slots, he hurried to help them set up the braces. The three of them finished the job together and stepped back, panting.

Jordan's eyes moved over the structure. The full length of the barn was now sketched against the sky. "What's next?"

"The girts," Kara murmured. "The beams that connect the bents about halfway up."

Jordan looked at his watch and let out a grunt. "I left John and Sabrina going over the brood mares with Mike. I've got to go pick them up." He scowled at her, then turned to Chris, his shoulders squared and stiff. "Haley, stay with her. Give her a hand." At Chris's grin of delight, his scowl intensified. Without another word he stalked away.

But he returned at five and silently fell into the building routine. By that time, Kara and Chris had lifted three girts into place with the help of the gin pole. With Jordan's assistance, the work went faster. They finished the fourth girt on the first side of the barn, then moved the gin pole around to the opposite side. Kara looked up from arranging the hand tools where they would need them, to see Mike Cavazos and Lew studying the day's work with critical approval. Then, apparently anticipating the next step, they walked to the nearest beam. Hefting it with a groan and a laugh, they brought it to where it was needed.

By the time the sun set, two more of the ranch hands had joined the crew. Jordan had lost some of his initial grimness, and Chris seemed to be losing his nervousness around his boss. Standing on a ladder, Kara pounded the final trunnel into the final joint, then turned around to grin at the men.

"That's it for the day," Jordan said quietly.

"Won't blow down now," Mike agreed.

They all turned to feast their eyes on the structure. It looked like a building now. Kara felt a swift rush of pride and gratitude. "Thanks, you guys!"

As they were putting away the tools, Chris touched her shoulder. "Kara, Lew tells me your dad's out by the high way."

"He is?" She straightened and turned to stare toward the road, as if she could see through the intervening hills.

"He told Lew he wants to see you. Said he'd wait there all night."

She was halfway across the barnyard before Jordan caught up to her in his car. He opened the passenger door. "How about a ride, carpenter?"

She didn't want to break the fragile harmony they'd found today on the job. But Hank, out there waiting in the dark . . .

"I'm not headed for the house, Jordan. Dad's out by the highway, I hear."

"Yes, Mike told me. Get in." When she hesitated, his voice sharpened. "In, Kara."

She slid in beside him. "You can't stop me from—"

"Who said I was? It's nearly a mile to the highway." He stomped down on the gas and the big car rumbled up the hill.

Kara looked back as they passed the house. There weren't many lights on in its lower rooms. "Where are the Dickersons?"

"Sabrina was getting bored. They've gone into San Antonio for some shopping."

Shopping. Kara felt a brief stab of envy. It would not be that hard to look sophisticated, if one had unlimited money for shopping. If only Jordan could see *her* in a five-hundred-dollar dress, he might stop thinking of her as just a kid. Forget it, she told herself sharply. "Did you sell them any stock?" she asked.

"We're working on it," Jordan murmured. "Dealing with John is like trading with an Iraqi rug merchant. We'll be days at this. He wants Dream..." He glanced at her sideways.

She swallowed and stared straight ahead. It was silly to feel so possessive about a horse she'd never owned. It was just that she'd broken Burning Dream in Jordan's company.... But maybe part of growing up was learning there were some dreams you never caught up with, however much you burned to make them real. She blinked rapidly, glad of the darkness. "That's nice," she said, forcing a note of indifference into her voice.

"Yes," he said heavily.

He stopped the Jag beneath the stone arch. Across the highway, a battered old van was pulled off the shoulder and parked. A warm light flickered behind it. "I'll wait," he said.

"I don't know how long—"

"I'll be here." He lounged down in his seat and crossed his arms.

He must be even more tired than she, she thought, looking at him. He should be laid up mending his bones, not working against the pain. She had to fight hard to control the urge to touch his lean cheek. "Thanks, Jordan."

Halfway across the empty highway, she recognized the van. It was an old one that Bubba Hendricks had driven for years, till it had died and been left to rust in his front yard with two or three other disintegrating companions. "Dad?" she called as she came around it.

"Kara!" He leaped from his seat in the sliding doorway of the van.

As Kara stepped into his bear hug, she felt as if it had been a month since they parted, not two days. "What are you doing here?" She looked around, taking in his campfire, an open can of Dinty Moore stew simmering in the coals, and a couple of milk crates for table and chair.

"Waiting for you. How do you like my new house? Bubba towed it out here for me."

Her eyes glazed with tears. "Dad, you don't have to do this."

"But I thought, if you needed me—needed to know what to do next..."

His expression reminded her of a stray dog that used to come to the kitchen screen door at some house they'd once rented. Every meal he'd been there. Wistful and polite, tail wagging, ready if someone just happened to have something they didn't want. "Oh, I do, Dad! I just finished the girts, and now I don't know what comes next."

The wistfulness faded to a satisfied smile. "Have you eaten yet?"

Somehow she'd pictured this night, sitting down to a table with Jordan. Not saying much to him—they were both too tired—but just sharing... What? she mocked herself. *Here you go hoping and wishing again—don't you ever learn?* And in the meantime, if Jordan didn't need or want her, here was someone who did. "I'd love that, Dad," she said softly. "Just let me go tell my ride."

Back at the car Jordan sat up as she came around to his window. "That was quick," he said. "Now what about some supper?"

"I'm going to eat with Dad, Jordan," she said quickly, "and get some advice about what to do next."

His smile straightened to a harsh line. "What makes you think there's going to be any next? What we did today had to be done. First windstorm, those temporary braces would have blown down."

Her hands clenched on the window frame. "Don't do this to me, Jordan. Come hell or high water, I'm building that barn. You know it, I know it."

"I know I'm damned if I'll sit here arguing, when I could be eating a hot steak in town," he snapped. "We'll talk about this later."

"Fine," she shot back. "We'll do that."

"Watch your toes." The Jag growled and spun gravel from its wheels as he stomped on the gas. Choking in its dust, Kara stared after it until its taillights rushed over a ridge and winked goodbye. Then, eyes watering, she trudged back across the highway.

CHAPTER ELEVEN

EARLY NEXT MORNING Jordan caught up with her in t[
kitchen. "One sugar, no cream," he said as he came up b[
hind her.

Coffee splashed on the counter as she spun around. He s[
an empty mug beside hers and frowned at her. In spite [
that look, she felt a smile as bright as the sunrise start[
dawn inside her. Turning before it broke, she filled his mu[

"What's the program today?" he asked while she su[
ared his coffee.

"*Lots* of mortising. I've got to make the plate beams [
These were the two lengthwise timbers that would cap all t[
bents, tying the whole structure together. Hank had draw[
her sketches and diagrams. But still . . . it wasn't going to [
easy.

"Tell me about it while you cook breakfast?" Jord[
suggested.

"Breakfast?" She glanced at the bread and cheese she[
meant to take with her.

Jordan picked her snack up and tossed it into the was[
basket under the sink. "Breakfast," he repeated. "You'[
going to have to feed your crew better than that if you wa[
a decent day's work out of him."

Wanting to hug him, not quite daring to, she turned h[
head to hide her smile. She studied the copper pots th[
hung from a beam—they were as bright as the feeling i[
side her. "How do you like your eggs?"

Lots of mortising, Kara thought ruefully some four hours later. She put down her corner chisel, then sat on the half of the plate beam she'd been working on. The barn was too long to make this beam from one timber. So it would be pieced together at the halfway point. She'd been putting off making the scarf joint that would connect the two halves all morning. Which was probably a mistake, she admitted to herself now. All her fine mortise cuts would be for nothing, if she could not make the two halves of the plate fit together properly.

"How're you doing?" Jordan put down the big saber saw he'd been using to make the rough cuts for her, then sat beside her.

She flexed her right hand within its clumsy work glove. "Hanging in there."

"Let's see." Catching her wrist, Jordan drew her work glove off. He sucked in his breath. "Ouch!" he muttered. A seam on the inside of the rawhide glove had been rubbing her all morning. The blister was already the size of a quarter. He let his breath out between his teeth and looked at her. "This'll only get worse, Kara. You've got to stop."

"No," she said and tried to draw her hand away.

"Little mule!" His fingers tightened warmly around her wrist. Gently he turned her hand over and studied the back of it, staring down at her slender fingers. "Is this—carpentry—what you want to do with your life?" he asked, without looking up again.

With the rest of her life? At the moment, sitting here having him touch her this way would have been enough. But that was not what he meant. With a sigh she looked over her shoulder at the barn. It was going to be beautiful. Solid. The biggest, most difficult accomplishment of her whole life. But as a way of life?

"No, it isn't," she said. "I've never been prouder o
anything I've done before, but . . . I want something *more*
Jordan, something different. I just don't know what yet
Maybe if I ever got an education, I'd figure it out?"

His smile was a strange one, tender and bleak all at once
"That's what growing up's all about, short stuff . . . figurin,
it out." He turned her hand, lifted it to his mouth and kisse
the blister.

A simple gesture—why should it bring tears to her eye
with its sweetness? But what he'd said needed answerin
even more than the caress. "Do you have to figure it all ou
before you're considered grown up, though? Maybe find
ing out what you want takes a whole lifetime, Jordan." An
she knew that this was the man she would want to have b
her side while she figured things out, no matter how long c
how hard that road might be, or where it led. Couldn't h
see that? Feel that himself?

But he didn't seem to be listening. "Maybe so," he mu
mured, sounding a thousand miles away. He changed th
subject. "How's your dad?"

"He's all right," she said cautiously. "He means to cam
there, in case I need him. That is, if the state troopers don
make him move on."

"They shouldn't. I lease that land for summer grazing.
I don't complain, I don't think they'll bother him."

So Hank was squatting there by Jordan's grace. Sh
should have known. Once, that would have rankled. No
she had to admit she was grateful. And she was encourage
enough to say, "About the other night . . ."

"Let's just forget it, can't we?" He stirred restlessly.

"There's something I want you to know—" She plowe
on in spite of his frown. And she went on to tell him abo
the bourbon and the toast Hank had never meant to drin

When she was done he sat there in silence, frowning. "If you say so, I'll believe it, Kara. But still... when he goes around making accusations like that, that I'd blind a horse—*any* animal—for money... A man's only as good as his name. When he starts saying things like that about me in public..." He shook his head.

"I don't know why you're always knocking my pride, Jordan Stonehall," she said quietly. "You've got enough to cover half of Texas yourself."

"I never said I didn't."

She should get up, go back to work, but it was so sweet, so rare, that they could simply talk. She pulled off her painter's cap and unclipped her hair, where it lay damp and hot against her neck. She put a hand under it to lift it off her nape.

His eyes swung to watch her. Then, moving so slowly he might have been hypnotized, he reached out to capture a strand of hair and wrapped its sun-silvered length around his finger.

When he tugged delicately, she could feel the sensation down to her toes. As if a thread of sunlight ran all the way through her, then bound them one to the other. "And what do *you* want from life?" she whispered.

A silent, rueful laugh feathered out of him, and he shook his head.

"What?" she coaxed. "I told you."

"Ohhh..." His eyes took on a faraway look as he twirled her lock of hair between thumb and middle finger. "I suppose I want more of the same, only better. I want to be here on the ranch, doing what I'm doing, but..."

"But?"

His mouth twisted suddenly, as if something tasted bitter. "I'm ready for a family, half-pint. Living alone, that's fine when you're running wild in your twenties. I wasn't

ready for marriage the last time I tried, any more than m
wife was. But I am now." His eyes veered to hers. There wa
nothing caressing about them now. They drilled right int
her, commanding her attention, daring her to blink or mis
understand. "So I'm looking for a woman. Someone wh
knows who she is and what she wants. Someone who's fin
ished her education, and is ready to settle down and raise
family."

And that wasn't her, he was telling her as clearly as h
knew how. She'd disqualified herself already with her ow
foolish mouth. She wanted to cry aloud that she would giv
up all her dreams of an education, of finding her place in lif
if he'd only love her, but something in his eyes told her he'
only smile sadly and turn away.

She swallowed hard—there was a lump in her throat tha
rose from nowhere. He was right, too—she wasn't ready
Not all the way. She'd take on Jordan in an instant, but he
children? Yes, oh, *yes*—someday. But now? She felt as
she'd been raising a child since she was twelve, taking ca
of Hank. She had no regrets, but she was so tired of bein
responsible. For just a few years she wanted to be a woma
alone with her lover. Light-hearted and free, sharing his lov
with no one. Was that so selfish?

He was unwinding her hair from his finger. Blinking bac
the tears, she stared at his hand. No, she wasn't being sel
ish, she was sure of that. It was just that the timing was s
wrong. So unfair. So *unanswerable*. Jordan needed som
one like Sabrina. He was right. He'd been right all along.

Jordan stood. "Guess we've got a barn to build." H
drew a knuckle along her bottom lip. "Come on, swee
heart, unless you're ready to give up?"

She shook her head fiercely. Maybe she couldn't grow u
overnight, but she could finish what she started. And sh

would. Taking the hand he held out to her, she rose to her feet and faced the barn.

By noon Kara's right hand was bleeding inside its glove. She'd been doing her best to ignore the pain, but Jordan noticed her biting her lip.

He demanded to see her hand again, then shook his head. "Quit, Kara."

"No."

His hand tightened on her fingers as if he wanted to crush them. "Admit it, you're beaten."

That was what he'd been waiting all morning for her to say, she realized, looking up at him. She shook her head.

He swore softly and dropped her hand. "Then you need a bandage." They turned together as a pickup, carrying Chris, Mike and several more of the hands, came rumbling down the hill from the direction of the bunkhouse. "Mike carries a first aid kit in his truck. I'll get it."

Kara stayed where she was, smiling at the lunch shift. But how was she going to use them today? She'd marked out the mortises to be cut in the other half of the plate, and Jordan had already rough cut them for her. But if she put the men to chiseling the mortises, what would she do?

Looking around, her eyes lighted on the saber saw. She'd been avoiding it. It scared her, truth to tell, though she'd certainly watched Hank use it often enough to know how it was done. But if she took over that chore, she could give the palm of her hand a rest, and lord knew it needed it.

Hoisting the heavy power tool, she walked over to the end of the plate. The lines along which the scarf joint would be cut were already drawn in chalk. Quite a large chunk of wood needed to be cut away to form this half of the joint. She could try a practice cut well inside the crucial lines.

She looked over her shoulder, found that Jordan and the men were still talking, but starting to turn in her direction.

Better to start now before she had a know-it-all male audience to laugh at her first mistakes. Holding her breath, she braced herself and squeezed the trigger. With a snarl the saw jerked to life in her hands, vibrating and flicking its big hungry blade in and out of the housing. The trick was to hold it steady, let the tool do the cutting, and not to twist the blade, whatever she did. Tensing her muscles, she set the blade down on the timber. It jumped, shrieked, then bit wood, slicing down through the beam as if it were butter.

She smiled and let it feed for a second. This wasn't so hard.

But it was cutting too fast, she realized suddenly. Another two inches and it would be slicing through the joint, severing material that must stay in place. She shut off the tool. It bucked in her hands and shrieked as it twisted slightly in the blade-thin slot it had created, then it stilled. Heart pounding, shaking slightly with the tension, she tried to pull the blade from the slot. It wouldn't budge. She could hear someone walking up behind her, but she didn't turn.

She'd made a mistake, she realized too late. The saw must be like an electric drill—much easier to withdraw while it was running. She squeezed the trigger again—and the saw shrieked and kicked like a wasp-stung mule. With a startled cry, she fought the machine, steadied it, then realized it was already over the line into good wood. "Stop it!" she cried. Lifting one foot, she braced it on the beam to steady herself and pulled upward. The saw resisted, then leaped in the slot—too fast. And at the last instant she must have twisted it. With a mechanical yell the blade lunged into view, bounced down on the top of the beam, chomped wood and rebounded. It landed on the edge of her work boot.

For half a heartbeat she stared in disbelief, then screamed and threw the saw from her. It shut itself off in mid-roar as her finger left the trigger, and her yelp rang out in the silence.

"Holy *Moses!*" Chris's hands clamped around her from behind as the saw crashed down. He swung her down on the beam. "Lemme see, Kara."

"I-I-I'm all right," she stuttered, as he knelt before her and lifted her boot onto his knee. Behind him she could see Jordan coming fast. She was all right now, but when he arrived, she was going to be nose-deep in trouble, that was as plain as the look on his face.

Flinching away from that scowl, she looked at her boot. Chris was touching it gingerly, pulling the slice that had been cut into the side of it away from the rest of the shoe.

"How bad is it?" Jordan landed on the ground next to Chris and pulled her foot away from him. He stared at the mangled leather in disbelief.

Had the cut been an eighth of an inch to one side, it would have sliced into flesh. As it was, the sole and the edge of the shoe had been sliced neatly through for three inches—her little toe and the side of her foot lay revealed like the delicate flesh inside the rind of a strange fruit. Jordan touched her skin, and a few drops of blood reddened his fingers.

"No more than a shaving cut," Chris said incredulously, while beside him Jordan started a string of curses the likes of which Kara had never heard before. The ring of men that had gathered widened hastily, and Kara found herself blushing beet red.

Finishing with an anatomically impossible suggestion that seemed to take in the barn, himself, the devil, and every airheaded, mule-minded female within fifty miles, Jordan lifted his eyes to glare at her.

She swallowed and tried to smile, then looked around her for help. But nobody here was going to take up for her, that was clear. Lew was scuffing wood chips, hands in pockets

and eyes on the ground. Mike looked disapproving, Chri
as if he wished he were in Oklahoma. She looked down a
Jordan peeled her boot off her foot. He lifted her foot, de
cided it was undamaged, then threw the boot as far as h
could.

His gaze returned to her foot, then shifted sideways along
the timber. He sucked in his breath.

That last struggle to free the blade had come too late
Realizing she'd sliced halfway through the joint, Kar
yelped in dismay. In one idiotic moment she'd ruined half
day's work.

Jordan dropped her foot, stood and whirled around t
glare at his foreman. "Mike, if she so much as *touches*
power tool..."

"She won't, boss," Mike said fervently. He cast Kara a
appealing glance.

"She'd better not!" Jordan stalked to the pickup, nearl
ripped its door off the hinges as he opened it, then backe
out of the barnyard with a roar and a cloud of dust. He wa
halfway up the hill to the big house before he remembere
to slam his door shut.

"Hooo—*eee*!" one of the men said admiringly.

Lew returned her boot to her, but Mike shook his head
"I don't know if I'd put that back on, Kara. It's just goin
to remind him."

Still blushing bright red, her eyes starting to water wit
reaction from Jordan's rage, she took the boot from Lew
"I've got nothing else to wear, Mike," she told him griml
and slipped it on. Her tennis shoes were at the big house
She quailed inwardly as she realized what would have hap
pened had she been wearing those lighter shoes today. Any
way, they were at the house, where she presumed Jordan ha
gone. She wouldn't have gone up there to fetch them righ
now for all the racehorses in Kentucky.

For the rest of the lunch hour, the men would not let her work. Instead she sat on the second half of the plate between Mike and Chris while they cut rafter mortises. From time to time her eyes strayed uphill, but she saw no sign of Jordan. Had he quit the project, just like that? She knew him well enough to know he must have hated losing his temper in front of her and the men. But would the damage to his pride be enough to drive him away from her and the barn?

With a sigh her eyes passed on to the ruined plate. She sighed again, and beside her Chris turned to see what she was looking at.

"You've got extra wood, don't you?" he asked comfortingly as he stopped to wipe the sweat from his eyes.

"Yes, I've got one standby timber left." But after she used that one, she could afford no more accidents. Suddenly, inexplicably, her eyes filled, and she looked away. She was so tired. So uncertain. How could she pretend that there would be no more accidents in construction, the way she was bumbling along? And Jordan had left her. Didn't want her.

"Here he comes," called Lew, looking up the hill.

Kara turned to see the pickup returning at a much saner pace than it had left, and she let out a breath of relief. His temper was back in control then. Not that that necessarily boded well for her, she realized on second thought. It might be that he'd been off clearing his head and deciding after this last accident to close down her project once and for all. If he'd come to that resolution in cold blood, she hadn't a prayer of changing his mind. Clenching her hands, she walked to meet him.

The sun reflected off the windshield and into her eyes. She lowered her lashes and lifted her chin. *You may not want me, Jordan Stonehall, but if you think I'm leaving this job, think again.*

But when the truck stopped, it was the passenger doo‹
that swung open. "Kara!" Her father slid into view an‹
hurried to meet her. "You okay, baby?" he asked as h‹
hugged her.

"I-I'm fine, Dad." Incredulously, she hugged him back
then looked beyond his shoulder as Jordan stepped out o›
the truck. His dark brows were pulled into a scowl. As thei›
eyes met, he shrugged and looked away. She turned t‹
Hank. "Does this mean—"

He was grinning ear to ear. "Yep, it means I'm back o›
the job! Now let's see what you've been up to."

A few minutes later, Kara left Hank figuring out how t‹
salvage the ruined plate beam and drifted over to Jordan›
"Thank you," she said with all her heart.

He grunted and hooked his thumbs into the pockets of hi‹
jeans. "Seemed easier than watching you kill yourself."

"He apologized for what he said, he tells me." And Hank
had also remembered that Jordan had saved her life, an‹
had thanked the rancher for that also. Between that an‹
Hank's gratitude at being reunited with his barn, a kind o›
peace had been negotiated—at least from his point of view›
Jordan looked less satisfied.

"Yes," he agreed. "But did he tell you the rest of ou›
deal?" When she shook her head, he went on. "No mor›
solo work. He gets five of my men to help him finish the job›
And you, my friend, are on the sidelines."

Her smile faded as the implications hit home. "But it'›
my barn, too!"

He caught her arm and pulled her closer. "And you ca›
do the light stuff, I don't say no to that, but no more risks›
Kara. That's carved in stone. Agree or I *will* boot you out.»

Her eyes started to fill, and the iron resolve in his fac›
softened. "Oh, Kara, don't take on that way. You're jus›

tired." His hand moved to the back of her neck, and his fingers curled around her, drawing her nearer.

Tears overflowing, blinking frantically, she looked away. But she didn't step back from that contact, though she felt as if it would break her heart. It had just hit her. With five men helping, they'd be through in no time. That was the point of all this, wasn't it? Jordan had had enough trouble from her. She and the barn-building had disrupted the whole pattern of his life. The sooner the barn was built, the sooner he could ease her out of his life and get on with his plans for the future. A future that had no place in it for her. She swallowed hard, fighting the tears, and his thumb curled round to the front of her throat to caress her.

"You still need a bandage," he said roughly. "Come on."

They were careful not to meet each other's eyes while he bandaged her hand. Kara was steeling herself, driving the sorrow down and inward into her soul, locking it out of sight until she could deal with it in merciful privacy. What Jordan was thinking, she could not have guessed. When he finished wrapping the last piece of tape, she muttered, "Maybe I'll take a break. Go pack my bag and take it down to the foaling barn."

His gray eyes swung up and moved to hers—a tangible presence, as if her heart had to fall back a step to make room for him inside her. "You don't have to move," he said. "I've got plenty of room. And you like the tub."

The tub was the least of the reasons she loved sleeping in the big house. Just sharing the same air with him . . . But if he didn't want her, then it was crazy for her to stay near him. She needed to put as much distance between them as possible. As soon as possible. She realized he was even right to use his men to hurry the barn's completion. Staying around him, seeing him, but not being able to touch him, to love him, would kill her slower than a falling piece of lumber.

But it would kill her just the same. "Thanks, anyway," she said faintly. "But Dad needs me. He can't cook anything but canned stew, and—"

Jordan dropped her hand and stood. "I get the picture," he said bleakly. "You're tied to him forever, aren't you?" He didn't give her a chance to answer but turned and walked away.

Sagging against the side of the pickup, Kara watched him go. No, she thought sadly, you've got that all wrong, Jordan. It's you I'm tied to.

Forever and aching ever.

WITH FIVE MEN helping, the barn almost seemed to build itself. It was like watching a misty dream slowly take on substance and solidity. Each day it became more real as the plate beams were hoisted into place and scarfed together. Then the rafters rose to draw their sharp peaks against the sky and to clasp the roof beam like prayerful hands.

But while the barn moved toward reality, Jordan became the dream. Now that Kara and Hank had sufficient help from his men, he no longer came to work. She caught only glimpses of him here and there—riding past with the Dickersons one day. Sitting his bay alone near sunset the next, to look up at her as she straddled the roof beam and nailed on shingles. When their eyes met, he touched his hat and reined his horse, then ghosted off beyond the trees. But if he was only a dream, he was a dream that burned deep within her, burning her thinner and sadder and quieter with each passing day.

It was on the fourth afternoon after Hank and Jordan had made their truce, that Kara looked down from the roof to see the Jag stopping in the barnyard. The Dickersons waved her a friendly salute as they left the car and strolled toward the barn. They vanished under the eaves of the roof then Jordan swung out of his door. For a moment he simply stood looking at her, then he looked away and started walking. As Kara watched, her father strode to meet him.

The two men stood talking, too low for her to catch their words. Hank's head jerked up in startlement, and he shook his head vigorously.

Jordan seemed to repeat his words, more forcefully this time, and again Hank rejected them. Kara caught her breath and looked to the ladder. Should she step into this dispute? She couldn't bear it if those two took to fighting again. Even though everything else about this job had been a heartbreaker, at least the end of Hank's grudge was cause for rejoicing.

Jordan took something out of his jeans and tucked it into Hank's shirt pocket. Hank snatched it out again, tried to hand it back, and now Jordan refused it, his hands held palm out as he shook his head.

Utterly mystified, Kara watched first Sabrina Dickerson then John return to join the altercation. Sabrina seemed to be mediating—or more accurately, charming the socks off Hank. As the woman spoke, Kara watched his posture change from indignant rejection to perplexity to a final reluctant acceptance. He shrugged, nodded sheepishly at Jordan and suddenly reached to shake his hand.

And then Sabrina led him away toward the barn, her slender hand hooked into the crook of Hank's arm. John grinned, said something to Jordan and ambled after the pair. Jordan stood looking after them, his face stern and thoughtful, as if a last debt had been paid, or a book closed.

His head tipped up, and their gazes meshed. Even at this distance the touch of his eyes was like a physical stroke across her face. Slowly he raised his good hand, touched his finger to his lips and held it out to her. *A kiss for you,* his eyes were saying. A kiss and farewell.

Her eyes filled, and she caught hold of the roof beam with both hands. *I could have loved you so, Jordan, if you'd let me.* When she could see again, the Jag was gliding toward the stables, slipping silently out of her life as a dream goes at dawn.

She stayed up there for a long time, trying hard not to feel. To be numb. She stared at the red sun, which was almost kissing the far-off hills, until she was blinded, then sat with her eyes closed until vision returned. Finally she climbed down from the roof.

Hank was standing outside the barn, staring uphill toward the stone house. In the distance Kara could see the Dickersons walking toward the crest. "What did they want?" she asked him.

"Hmmm? Ohh!" He woke from his daze and turned toward her, and slowly a smile spread. "They wanted a tour of the barn." His smile widened to a grin. "They thought we're doing some job."

"We are," Kara agreed and looked at the building. Another week and it would be done. The walls and roof were closed in, most of the floor was laid, they were down to the details and the interior joiner work. A week and she'd have no more excuse to clutter up Jordan's life.

"Matter of fact they liked it *so* much—" Hank caught Kara's waist and hand in a dance grip and waltzed her twice around. "They liked it so much that they want us to come up to Connecticut! Seems the brother—John—has been planning himself a fancy post and beam house for some time now. He's got the architect, and he's been shopping for his builder. What do you say, partner—want to see how the Yankees live?"

"Dad! That's wonderful!" Somehow she put some heart into her words, while inside her a voice was crying, *Connecticut!* It might have been at the ends of the earth, sounded so far. But she hugged him back anyway. "A commission! And what a commission, Dad. Those folks are loaded. I'm sure it'll be a lovely house."

"And who's to say it'll stop with one house?" Hank was off and dreaming already. "They aren't having the hard times we're having here, Kara. We build one dynamite house, maybe—well, one thing leads to another. We may just decide we like it there, and stay, if business is good. Who can say?"

A year ago, what she would have given to hear him say he'd leave Texas! A year ago, he could have dreamed it, but he would never have had the confidence to do it. She nodded, the smile frozen on her face. But Hank was too excited to see her pain.

"Oh! And that's not all." He scrounged in his pocket and pulled out a folded paper. "Look at this, will you!" He held it out to her.

It was a check for forty-seven thousand dollars, made out to Jordan Stonehall. As her eyes rounded, he turned it over. In a big, angular hand that Kara knew instinctively was Jordan's own, the fire insurance check had been endorsed on the back, and the additional words added, "Pay to the order of Hank Tate".

"Course we'll want to pay the crew out of this," Hank was saying. "I can't see letting Stonehall pay them for this week when they were working for us, but still, baby—we're rich!"

"Jordan gave you that . . . ?" Kara said faintly.

"Sure did! I tried to tell him we couldn't take it, but he kept on insisting. Said he didn't need it, that he was back where he started, only better, with his barn ten years newer now. And that sweet little Miss Dickerson said—"

"Do you know where he went?" Kara asked suddenly.

Hank looked at her, and his blissful grin graduall[]
sharpened. He ducked his head to peer at her intently.

"Where, Dad?" she demanded.

"He didn't say, honey. He went that-a-way." Hank nod[]
ded toward the stables.

Chris had driven into town with some of the other hand[]
and had left his Jeep parked by the barn. Its keys were in th[]
ignition, and she took it without a qualm. She had to se[]
Jordan. Now.

Eyes sweeping the landscape, she drove past the foalin[]
barn, then the brood mare stables. The track was empty o[]
horses and men at this hour, and the Jag was nowhere i[]
sight. At the bunkhouse, Lew lounged on the front porch[]
a cigarette between his lips. When she asked, he hooked [ ]
thumb toward the road. "He headed for Joe's."

She parked the Jeep far from the paddock and walked th[]
rest of the way. Peering through the fence rails, she sa[]
them. Jordan was lunging Smoky Joe on a long rope, th[]
great white stallion wheeling in wide circles around th[]
slowly pivoting man. They'd been at it for a while, sh[]
judged. In the late slant of golden light, the stud's coat wa[]
darker at chest and shoulders with his sweat. But h[]
breathed easily, his ugly ears pricked with pleasure. The lon[]
lash that Jordan held, he held upright and forgotten. Th[]
stallion rotated on his lunge line with gigantic, flowin[]
strides, a force of nature, like the moon rounding the earth.
A cosmic clock that would never run down.

Jordan's eyes were fixed on the stud, but his face held n[]
pleasure or awe at the sight of him. Only a stillness and [ ]
waiting.

He saw Kara as she neared the stud, and he lifted his chi[]
in warning, but on she came. She waited until Joe spotte[]
her, as his good eye came into play on the far side of th[]

circle. Waited until he'd swept past her with an acknowledging snort, then she stepped into his orbit.

"Kara!" Jordan called warningly, but she walked on, her eyes on the oncoming lunge line. She crouched to let it pass overhead, then continued.

"I told you to never come in here," he growled as she reached him.

"Without you," she reminded him, pivoting shoulder to shoulder with him to face the stallion. Then as he lifted the lunge line to signal a halt, she said quickly, "No, Jordan, let him run. Please?"

Wordlessly he dropped his whip and drew her in front of him. His arm encircled her waist, and he pulled her snugly against him, her back molded to his front. Over her shoulder, he watched the running stallion while his left hand held the lunge line.

Yes. Shivering with contentment, a moving part of his world, she rotated with him, her eyes on that mesmerizing beauty, her heart filled to overflowing. The thunder of Joe's hooves merged with the thunder of Jordan's heart against her shoulderblade. When he kissed the side of her jaw, she arched her neck and put up a hand to cup his cheek.

He sighed, and his arm tightened around her until she groaned with pleasure. "Kara," he growled, rubbing his face through her hair, "What am I going to do with you?"

Love me, she thought as they spun in their slow dance with the stallion. *Just please, please, love me.*

Lifting his head, he whistled. Joe flicked an ear their way and began to slow. She didn't want this to stop, not ever, but Jordan whistled again. The stallion halted and turned inward to face them, then, as Jordan tugged the line, he walked to meet them.

As he loomed above them, Joe was breathing easily, the deep, smooth breaths of a conditioned athlete. Jordan un-

clipped the line to his halter and dismissed him with an a[b]
sent slap to the shoulder.

But the stud didn't move. He thrust his nose into Kara[']
face and inhaled gustily. Laughing, rubbing her chee[k]
against his nuzzling velvet, she ran a hand up his prou[d]
neck. "Yeah, you remember me, don't you?" she mu[r]
mured fondly.

Jordan laughed and pushed him away, then slapped h[is]
shoulder again. "Forget it, fella! She's mine." This time th[e]
stud snorted, shook his ugly head and flowed away.

She's mine. Watching him go, Kara felt her eyes pric[k]
with tears. If it were only so! Then Jordan swung h[er]
around to face him.

"What did you come out here for?" he asked bluntly.

"To thank you." Because she couldn't stay away. B[e]
cause she had nothing left to lose but her pride, and she'[d]
give up even that, if— Reaching up to his lean face to cup [it]
with her hands, she stepped as close as she could and ro[se]
against him on tiptoe. "Thank you," she whispered. H[er]
lips touched his in a kiss that started lightly as the brush [of]
a butterfly wing. But it deepened as they both groaned wit[h]
delight and closed their eyes. Then, as Jordan's arm[s]
wrapped around her and hugged her to his heart, it dee[p]
ened even more. Kara felt as if she were falling—falling i[n]
ward and upward. Soaring toward everything she'd ev[er]
wanted or needed.

Her arms slid up around his neck. Breasts flattened to hi[s]
chest, thighs pressed to thighs, she stayed there. This was a[s]
close to heaven as she'd ever come. She was darned if she'[d]
let him go!

Finally their lips moved apart. Jordan's breathing raspe[d]
as loud as his stallion's. "Thank me for what—the check?["]
he asked, his voice rough with passion. She nodded, cares[s]

ing his cheek with the tip of her nose as she did so, and he smiled. "Ah . . . but that check's for your dad, not you."

All she cared about was this moment. "Doesn't matter."

His hand found her hair clip and snapped it open, freeing her hair. He plunged his fingers into it. "You, I have something different for. Or two things. You'll have to choose which you want."

She wanted only him—told him so again with her kiss. When they could breathe again, he said, "I kept Dream for you, if you want her. I'll race her for you if you like, or she can be your riding mare. And she can stay here if you've no place to keep her."

It was generous, even more generous than what he'd given her father, but not what she wanted at all. Couldn't he see that? With a little sigh of despair, she rested her forehead against his chest.

"Not what you wanted?" he whispered at her ear, then nuzzled her till she shivered. Hugging him closer, refusing to lift her head, she shook it against him.

"Then what *do* you want, Kara Tate?" he asked her and kissed her temple.

Her arms tightened, telling him, but that wasn't good enough. She lifted her head to look him in the eye. He'd wanted a woman who knew what she wanted from life? "You," she said simply.

"That was your other choice." His sexy, beautiful mouth didn't smile as he returned her gaze. "But it comes with some long strings. You know what I want. I want someone who won't run out on me when the going gets tough. Someone who'll stay here and build a life with me."

All her hope, all her passion rang out in her words. "You think I don't know how to build? And you *know* I don't quit what I start, Jordan!"

His mouth curled ever so slightly. "You don't quit build ings— I've learned that for sure. But people, Kara? Me? That's what I've been pondering all week. That's what planned to ask you tonight."

"Jordan, try me!" She stroked his cheek with the back of her fingers. "I *promise* you . . ."

Laughing softly, he moved his face against her caress "And when a Tate gives her word, yes, I know." He pulle a shaky breath, then let it out slowly. But when he spok again, his voice had hardened subtly. "What about you dad?"

She met his steel gray gaze, then tore her eyes away. Sh stared at his shirtfront, trying to think. Her father . . . If sh left him now, when he was just gaining his feet . . . Jordan fingers caught her chin, and he tipped her face to meet h searching eyes. "I love my father," she said, her voic trembling. "I won't deny that."

"And I'd never ask you to. But can you let him go, Kara I won't have a daddy's girl."

It hurt. It felt as if he were asking her to pull an old liv oak up by its roots. She could see her father's face as she' last seen it, shining with hope and triumph.

"I'm asking, can you forsake all others?" Jorda prompted relentlessly.

But she had. Already. There would never be anyone fo her but this man, no arms but these that held her. She coul no more deny that, than she could tell the sun not to rise And knowing Hank, she knew there was no way he'd wa her to deny it.

She pictured Hank's face and saw the strength behind th happiness. If she cut the string, he wouldn't fall now. He' fly as high as a kite. He'd build himself a future, with her o without. She took a deep breath. "I will," she said, he words a promise and a vow.

His arms hardened in swift possession as his mouth relaxed, but he wasn't done asking yet. "And our babies?" His chest moved against her breasts then stilled, as if he'd caught a breath and held it.

Was this the final test? If she answered this wrong... But if they were truly talking of a partnership here, then nothing less than the truth would do. "You'd have to wait for a while. Make do with me. Say six years?"

"Five," Jordan countered so quickly that she knew he'd had that answer waiting.

Laughter shivered inside her, made her voice shaky as she said, "You've got yourself a deal!" Then she bit her lip.

"What else?" he asked and swept the hair off her forehead.

"I'm going to have to to go to school... You wouldn't want to have an uneducated wife—not for long. I'll get a scholarship, or a loan."

He snorted, then rested his forehead on hers. "I'll lend you the money, ma'am, long as you can handle the interest," he said in a silky drawl.

"Ohhh...I think I can handle it." She smiled, held his eyes, and then was held by them, was pulled forward inexorably until their mouths joined and their breath became one. When they parted this time, she was so dizzy that she had to lean against him.

"But there's a condition that goes with that loan," he growled into her hair. "You come home to me nights. I'll teach you how to fly, if you mean to commute to Austin or San Antone, but nights I want the woman I love home."

Home. The word rang in her heart like a great golden bell. Like a dream risen up and made real. Strong enough to last a hundred years, if no fool burned it down. And no fools here, Kara thought, as their lips touched again. No fools, only two lucky, lucky, lucky people.

EPILOGUE

CHRIS HALEY stopped short in the bunkhouse doo "Hank, what are you doing here? I thought you were dri ing the bride to church?"

Hank looked at his new suit, one that Kara had picke out for him the previous week. "I am. Just got somethir I've got to do first. Won't take but a minute." Hoisting tl box he hugged in his arms a little higher, he sidled past Chr and walked into the big, comfortable living room that tl single men shared.

Chris followed him inside. "We're leaving, ourselves, a minute, if Lew ain't drowned himself in the shower. He you wouldn't know where the boss means to park his ca would you? We rounded up a couple of dozen old boots ar some tin cans and the shaving cream. And Mrs. Cavaz gave us all the rice we'll need."

"Nah, Jordan's playing cagey about that car," Har said, peering to right and left as he strolled into the kitche His eyes swept the room. "He left for town a few minut ago. I 'spect he'll hide it somewhere."

"We'll find it," Chris declared. He studied the older ma his frank blue eyes betraying his puzzlement. But if Har wanted to tell him what he was up to, he would witho prodding. "You decided when you're heading for Conne ticut yet?"

"Next week." Hank set his box on the counter and looke around again. "There's a couple of guys I used to work wit who I'm taking along— Bill and Eddy. They're finishing a project up in Dallas—then we'll all drive up together.''

"That's good,'' Chris said approvingly. ''You won't miss your right-hand gal so much, with some buddies along.''

"Oh, I'll miss her all right, but take one look at her face now'days, and you know I'm doing the right thing. You don't raise 'em to keep 'em. You raise 'em to watch 'em fly....'' His eyes far away, Hank rubbed the top of his shiny head, then he looked nervously around the room again.

Lew stopped in the doorway, his hair wet and slicked back from the shower. ''Let's get a move on!'' he announced, looking from one to the other of the men. Chris nodded and sauntered toward the door.

"Chris?'' Hank's face looked a shade pinker in the kitchen light. ''You haven't seen that ol' barn cat and her kittens, have you? I brought 'em a wedding day treat.''

Chris blinked, but he moved into the room and headed for the refrigerator. ''I reckon they're sacked out on Mike's bed, if I know those critters. But here's how you call 'em.'' He opened and closed the refrigerator door smartly two or three times.

As light hurried footsteps pattered toward the kitchen, Chris left the room again, calling back over his shoulder, ''Now you make sure you get the bride to church, you hear? Wouldn't be much of a wedding without her.''

"I'll say,'' Hank told the mama cat and her two half-grown kittens as they mewed and rubbed against his ankles. Quickly he pulled a can of tuna from his box, opened it and forked it into a bowl. Then, careful not to trip on the weaving cats, he walked to the kitchen pantry, opened the door and set the bowl on the floor. The cats surged through the doorway, sniffed at the bowl, then hunched down and set to.

Taking a smaller box full of sand out of his big box, Hank
set that inside the pantry also, and then a water dish. A
doubtful frown on his face, he looked down at the cats, then
he patted the mama gingerly on her soft side. Stepping out
of the pantry, he shut the door behind him, then for good
measure, propped a chair under the doorknob.

He took a hand-lettered sign out of the box and tacked it
onto the pantry door. It said:

"Absolutely, positively, do *not* let these cats out, till the
barbecue at the barn is over! Thank You."

That taken care of, he glanced at his watch, then headed
out the door.

HARLEQUIN
Romance®

Coming Next Month

#3103 TO TAME A COWBOY Katherine Arthur
Jennifer needed to get away from the city, her parents' bickering and a violent
boyfriend. A ranch in Montana seems far enough, her new boss Clay Cooper a warm
generous man. Jennifer begins to relax until she finds herself an unwilling
participant in another family's row!

#3104 CITY GIRL, COUNTRY GIRL Amanda Clark
Stung by a bee, knocked down by a huge muddy dog—that's Hannah's introduction
to country life. So the last thing she expects is to actually *enjoy* the enforced
vacation. Or to fall in love with a country vet named Jake McCabe....

#3105 THE GIRL WITH GREEN EYES Betty Neels
When Lucy meets eminent pediatrician William Thurloe, she determines to become
the woman of his dreams. The fact she is neither clever nor sophisticated like Fiona
Seymour, who wants William, too, is just one small obstacle she has to overcome.

#3106 OF RASCALS AND RAINBOWS Marcella Thompson
Kristy Cunningham races to Mount Ida, Arkansas, to find her missing grandfather.
She runs up against her granddad's young partner and self-proclaimed protector—
and the strangest feeling that she must stay, no matter what....

#3107 THE GOLDEN THIEF Kate Walker
Leigh Benedict seems to think every young aspiring actress is a pushover for the
casting couch, and his cynical attitude appalls Jassy. But the attraction that flows
between them makes it difficult for her to convince him otherwise.

#3108 THAI SILK Anne Weale
Clary helps a fellow Briton in trouble in Thailand by summoning Alistair Lincoln
halfway around the world to bail out his stepsister. But when he insists on Clary
sharing responsiblity for young Nina, it's Alistair who becomes the problem.

**Available in February wherever paperback books are sold, or through
Harlequin Reader Service:**

In the U.S.
901 Fuhrmann Blvd.
P.O. Box 1397
Buffalo, N.Y. 14240-1397

In Canada
P.O. Box 603
Fort Erie, Ontario
L2A 5X3

Harlequin Intrigue®

REBECCA YORK

Labeled a "true master of intrigue" by *Rave Reviews*, best-selling author Rebecca York makes her Harlequin Intrigue debut with an exciting suspenseful new series.

It looks like a charming old building near the renovated Baltimore waterfront, but inside 43 Light Street lurks danger . . . and romance.

Let Rebecca York introduce you to:

> *Abby Franklin*—a psychologist who risks everything to save a tough adventurer determined to find the truth about his sister's death. . . .
>
> *Jo O'Malley*—a private detective who finds herself matching wits with a serial killer who makes her his next target. . . .
>
> *Laura Roswell*—a lawyer whose inherited share in a development deal lands her in the middle of a murder. And she's the chief suspect. . . .

These are just a few of the occupants of 43 Light Street you'll meet in Harlequin Intrigue's new ongoing series. Don't miss any of the 43 LIGHT STREET books, beginning with #143 LIFE LINE.

And watch for future LIGHT STREET titles, including #155 SHATTERED VOWS (February 1991) and #167 WHISPERS IN THE NIGHT (August 1991).

HI-143-1

Coming soon
to an easy chair near you.

FIRST CLASS is Harlequin's armchair travel plan for the incurably romantic. You'll visit a different dreamy destination every month from January through December without ever packing a bag. No jet lag, no expensive air fares and *no* lost luggage. Just First Class Harlequin Romance reading, featuring exotic settings from Tasmania to Thailand, from Egypt to Australia, and more.

FIRST CLASS romantic excursions guaranteed! Start your world tour in January. Look for the special **FIRST CLASS** destination on selected Harlequin Romance titles—there's a new one every month.

NEXT DESTINATION:
THAILAND

 Harlequin Books

JTR2